John Marsden's lov[...] began in his early primary school years. [...] books then were *The Children of Cherry Tree Farm*, *Robinson Crusoe* and everything by Nan Chauncey. By Grade 4 he was writing stories for a class news-paper, an early experience with publication that left a happy impression on him.

His first novel wasn't published until he was 37, but since then he's become one of Australia's most successful writers for young people. He's currently working on a trilogy; the first volume of which was *Tomorrow, When the War Began*. The second volume, *The Dead of the Night* will be released in October 1994.

John now lives in Sandon, via Newstead, Victoria, but is often found in motels and airports, as he travels around Australia taking writing workshops.

Of *The Journey* he says 'This is the way the world should be, and very nearly is. I'm proud of this book.'

Also by John Marsden in Pan

THE JOURNEY

JOHN MARSDEN

PAN
AUSTRALIA

First published in hardback 1988
First Pan edition published 1989 by Pan Macmillan Pty Limited
St Martins Tower, Level 18, 31 Market Street, Sydney

Reprinted 1991, 1992, 1994 (twice), 1995

National Library of Australia
cataloguing-in-publication data:

Marsden, John
The journey
ISBN 0 330 27171 7
I. title.
A823'. 3

Printed in Australia by McPherson's Printing Group

TO A GOOD FRIEND,
WHO IN MANY DIFFERENT WAYS
INSPIRED THIS BOOK

ACKNOWLEDGEMENTS

Though I've known much kindness from many people in recent years, some have given me particular help in writing this and other books, and I'd like to thank them here. They include the Austin family of 'Mundarlo', the Laycock family of Khancoban, the Madin family of Christ Church Grammar, the Montague family of 'Osterley', the Rose family of Mosman, the Utz family of Mosman, and especially, Mary Edmonston, of all over the place. And I thank my own family very much for their support and loyalty.

A voyage that never leaves shelter
Is one for the weak and the small.
The strength a ship has, comes from its fight
To weather the rips and the rocks and the squalls...

Chapter One

Every year Argus asked his father, 'Is it time yet? Am I old enough?' And every year his father replied, 'No, you've got a while yet' or 'No, sorry son'. The first few times he laughed as he said it, as though the question were a droll one to be asked by someone of his son's age. But as Argus grew older his father ceased to smile and instead answered irritably, as if he didn't want to think about the matter. Perhaps though, his impatience was a reflection of his son's; for every year Argus put the question in a more insistent tone, feeling guilty as he did so, but driven strongly to ask.

Once, Argus tried to gain some insight into his father's mind, and in so doing to bring about a change in his attitude. He asked him, 'Why do you think I'm not ready?' But his stern father, busy trimming a new curb for a horse, replied briefly, 'You can't even do your jobs around here properly. I asked you two days ago to fix that fence in North Austin.' And after a moment's silence the boy walked away, trying to maintain his dignity. He was too proud to say that he had fixed the fence when asked, but a fox had made a new hole in it overnight, three panels along from the repair.

One afternoon, when Argus had just turned fourteen,

he and his father were working in South Austin, checking for cows that might have calved in the long grass, and tagging the ones they found. Argus held a wet and slippery new calf between his legs while its anxious mother hovered nearby. Somehow the calf got the boy slightly off-balance; sensing its advantage it twisted, bucked, flung its head and escaped, treading heavily on Argus' father's foot as it fled. Argus was buffeted about the face and body by a storm of angry words as his father raged. Knowing his father had lost his grip on two calves one morning just a week earlier, the boy said nothing. For the rest of the day the two worked together in silence, each reliving the argument in his mind, each trying to convince himself he was right. The unease between them lasted through the evening.

It was this incident that convinced Argus his time had come. In recent months he had been asking his father not 'Am I old enough?' but 'How soon before I go?' Now he decided he must take matters into his own hands; yet so great was his awe, love, fear and anger that it was three more days before he was able to speak of his decision. Finally, one night as his parents were folding astronomy charts, he told them.

Their reaction was an anti-climax: they both barely hesitated, but went on with their tasks, until his mother asked, 'When do you want to start?'

'At the end of the week,' he replied, trying to keep his voice steady.

'You can't go,' his father said. 'I'll need you for the harvest.'

But Argus was prepared for this. 'You can use Ranald again, the same as you did when I was ill.'

No more was said that night; no more was said on the subject for two days following. But on the eve of his going, his father brought Argus the book from its glass case, and placed it in his hands. 'You'd better read it,' he said, 'and then it will be time for us to talk.'

Argus was not able to look at his father, but instead watched his own hands, damp on the soft leather, as the silver-haired man left the room. And the boy, full of nervous excitement, began at last to read.

Argus learned from the book that there were seven stories, and the journey would not be over until he had discovered and could tell all seven of them. The seven stories that he found would be uniquely his, yet they would also be the stories of all people — the same for everyone, recognisable by everyone. The harder he searched, the more difficult the stories would be. The book warned him that nothing was simple: everything was complex, whether it be a leaf, a human, an idea, a word. Even the statement that nothing was simple was too simple, and was probably not wholly true. For the book also warned him that there were no absolutes; such extreme terms as good and evil, true and false, alive and dead, might be convenient words, but should only be seen as indications, not as definitions.

Argus read slowly, trying to understand and remember everything. He felt his mind opening up to infinite possibilities, yet at the same time he was disappointed that there were no practical directions in the book. His mind was sated but his body was restless. The book seemed to assume throughout that the journey was dangerous; it was implied in every sentence. Yet there was no indication of the form the danger might take, nor any suggestion of how to overcome it.

His father was of more practical help, though still vague. 'You take what you choose, and go where you choose,' he said when he came back into the room. 'What you take and where you go will tell you a good deal about who you are. Each item you pack will slow you down with its weight. If comfort is important to you, then you might take toilet paper. If safety is important to you, take bandages. If time matters, then take a clock. But remember, speed is not everything. The slow traveller sees detail.' He laughed. 'But as for me, I always regretted not taking toilet paper.'

Chapter Two

W hen Argus left, mid-afternoon, he was surprised
to find that it was his father who seemed most
affected. His mother was grave, almost det-
ached, but his father could hardly speak and, as Argus
hugged him, his eyes filled with tears. Argus strode away.
To his disappointment his dog, whom he had imagined
would have to be chained up to stop him following, did
not even notice him go.

His father had told Argus that everything he saw would
be important and should be noted. Knowing this made
Argus more observant. He felt fresh and aware and,
although he was still in familiar country, he found himself
seeing things he had never seen before. The way in which
a tree seemed to have one side dominant over the other.
And the apparent symmetry of a tree concealed so much
internal variation and chaos. 'Trees don't bother about
how big or small they are,' Argus realised with some
surprise, thinking about how he had worried lately about
his own size and shape. 'They just keep growing upward
and outward until they've finished. They're beautiful, no
matter what.'

But for Argus, who had been living in the country for
almost as long as he could remember, it was the towns

and villages that were exerting a powerful influence on him now. He wanted to mix with crowds of people, to meet strangers and to smell their sweat, to hear their conversations and to watch their faces. He was intensely curious. He quickened his pace, not to get to some unknown destination more quickly, but simply to get away from the valley that he knew and the sights to which he had been long accustomed.

At around dusk he passed through the town of Random where his parents did their trading. He did not pause, but was aware of the curious stares of the adults in the street, who knew at once what he was about, but were forbidden by the strongest customs (those who knew him) to speak or wave to him, as he was forbidden to speak or wave to them. But he felt no inclination to jeopardise his new independence by doing so.

Argus walked on into the night. He took apples from an orchard and ate them as he went, and then had some bread from his pack. He wasted twenty minutes trying to pick some blackberries in the dark. Although he succeeded in picking quite a number, he did not find them particularly filling, and the scratches were discouraging. Nevertheless the food he had eaten gave him the energy to climb the pass out of the valley. He topped it at around midnight, with a sense of tired triumph, and soon afterwards dropped down into a gully, where he rolled himself up in his blanket and, trying to ignore the shuffles and whispers of the night, closed his eyes and fell asleep. He slept well. A few times he woke to change position when his hip became uncomfortable, but he quickly went back to sleep each time.

In the morning he was hungry, but he knew from experience that the hunger would pass; he ignored it and climbed back up to the road to resume his travels. Once he had walked off his early-morning stiffness he was again able to set a good pace. He was still in a valley that he knew, but he had not been this far often and he kept onwards with a growing sense of excitement.

In the early afternoon he passed the gate that led to the Kakas' farm; this property, belonging to friends of his parents, marked the limit of his known territory. From this point on, although the landscape had not changed significantly, the boy was vividly aware that each stone and each tree, each view of the distant mountains, was new and fresh to his eyes.

When he bedded down, at a comparatively early hour, Argus had spent a day with virtually no human contact, though he was hardly aware of the fact. He had been yelled at by a distant farmer, when he hopped a fence to pick some sunflower seeds, but he had met no-one on the road. As well as the sunflower seeds, he had eaten more bread and blackberries, and had stolen some potatoes from a paddock. That evening, for the first time, he lit a fire, for comfort mainly, but also to cook the potatoes. He lacked the patience, however, to wait for the fire to settle down into the coals that he needed for cooking; as a result, he ate the potatoes half-raw.

He lay that night looking up at the stars. As the fire faded and its light dimmed, Argus' night sight improved, and he was able to discern more and more stars, until the black sky was richly alive with them: a staggering coruscation spread across the dark backdrop like huge numbers of glow-worms in a cave. 'Perhaps that's what I'm living in,' Argus thought, 'a cave with a ceiling that keeps changing colour... and all those stars are really insects... friendly insects, though.' He turned over and considered another problem. 'If it takes the light from the stars years to reach us, then when I look at the stars now, I'm actually seeing the past... it's a fire that was burning millions of years ago, and might have gone out hundreds of thousands of years ago, but I'm seeing it now. Not a picture of it but the actual thing, a fire that's actually out.' He asked himself another question: 'Is this the only time we ever get to see the past?' He realised then with a shock that, because light takes time to travel, everything he saw was already something from the past, had already happened.

His mind drifted on, to think of incidents from his own life. One of his first memories was of being in the house alone one afternoon and lighting a fire on his bedroom floor because he was cold. He remembered how he carefully assembled and ignited the kindling, and got a small but cheerful blaze going. He remembered the reaction when his mother found him and the chaos as the fire was extinguished. Later, when everyone had calmed down, his grandmother said to him, 'You know, your father did exactly the same thing one day when he was your age. Nearly burnt the house down.' Now he wondered, 'Is everything new, everything that happens? Is it like walking down a road where you can't go backwards, or is it like I pick moments out of a big collection of moments, and relive them? The way a parrot picks at seeds on the ground?' As he drifted into sleep he began dreaming of a huge library of books, in which men and women and children were constantly taking down the volumes from the shelves, and glancing at them, or browsing through them, or reading them thoroughly, and then replacing them. Some books would then be immediately taken down by someone else; some would sit back on their shelves for quite a time before being touched again; but all the books were handled more than once by the people in the library.

In the morning Argus was hungry, but he was anxious not to eat too much from his pack, and so he pressed on. The land was opening out now into a flatter, more arable terrain, different from the valleys in which he had spent his childhood. Away to his right, on the distant horizon, was a thin column of black smoke. Around mid-morning Argus came to a gate and driveway that clearly led to a farmhouse; without much hesitation he opened the gate and walked up the drive to the house. Dogs barked at him as he approached, but as soon as he made friends with one, the others forgot their hostility and they all ran to him, fawning and licking and snuffling. An old man came out of a shed and looked at Argus who had prepared his speech and now delivered it.

'I was wondering if I could do some work in exchange for a good meal?' he asked, immediately pursing his lips in exasperation at himself. He had not meant to say 'good'. It sounded rude, as though he were suggesting that the farmer might offer people bad meals. It was his first real contact with another person since leaving home, and his voice already sounded a little hoarse through lack of use. But the farmer appeared to notice nothing. He came closer, and Argus realised that he had some paralysis down one side of his body; it had even dragged at half his face and warped it out of shape.

'Well, you can chop some wood,' the old man said, without much hesitation. 'It's always a useful thing to have wood chopped.' He looked more critically at Argus. 'Have you had any breakfast?' he asked. 'Maybe we better pay you in advance.'

'No, I'm fine,' Argus said. 'I'd be happy to chop wood, if you can just show me where it is.'

The boy chopped wood for nearly two hours, ignoring the sharp and petulant messages from his belly. He wondered why it was more pleasant to chop wood for strangers than for one's own fireplace, and he was intrigued by the small differences between this woodpile and the one to which he was accustomed. This stack was neater than the one at home, for example, and the wood was cut into shorter lengths. The bark had been stripped from it and had been stacked in a separate pile. Argus chopped at a steady pace, amusing himself by seeing how high he could make the chips fly, trying to land them in a small bird's nest at the top of a nearby bush. But the pile of chopped pieces steadily grew, and the old man, when he returned, was pleased. 'Seems like you've earned breakfast and lunch' he commented, leading the boy into the wash-house.

When they entered the kitchen, Argus was surprised by the number of people there. He was introduced to them all and, despite some confusion, managed to gather that the youthful looking woman at the stove was the old farmer's wife, and that the others were sundry children, grandchildren and farmhands. There were fourteen or fifteen people in all, and their rowdy chatter relieved Argus of the need to say very much, for which he was grateful. They ate soup with hunks of bread, and followed it with a kind of fish stew, containing flavours that were unfamiliar to Argus.

The boy was almost overwhelmed by the rich odours and tastes, after several days of plain living. He was enjoying, too, the warm sound of the people crowded around the table, and he accepted with pleasure the old man's offer of an evening meal and a bed for the night, in exchange for help with roofing a shed. He worked on the shed with one of the old man's sons, a dark-bearded fellow named Rastam, and Rastam's two little daughters, Xenia and Narlan. The two girls worked earnestly and well; Rastam worked well too, but with a constant stream of witticisms and practical jokes, which Argus found alternately irritating and amusing.

After dinner the food was cleared away and the dishes were washed. The children began a game that they called, for no reason that Argus could fathom, 'Butterflies'. It seemed to be a guessing game based on imitations. One child would jump on the table and impersonate, with appropriate noises and contortions of the face and body, an object or creature; a parrot, for example, or a chair, and the others would try to guess what it was. The children were very skilful, both in their acting and in their guessing. To Argus' surprise, after ten minutes or so, the adults began joining in. Argus, accustomed to the gravity of his father and mother, was confused but pleased as the game spread through the room. And no-one was more active and rowdy than the old man, who, ignoring his paralysis, seemed to shed sixty years. He impersonated, in turn, the little girl Narlan, a baby pig, and a travelling wool-trader, and he imitated each one with wonderful accuracy. Argus was enchanted. But no-one could guess his last character, as he sat motionless on a chair, gazing into the fire. The guesses ranged from 'a rock' to 'a spirit'. At last everyone gave up and the old man cackled with glee, 'Myself! I was being myself!' before he toddled off to bed. They could hear him giggling and wheezing all the way up the stairs.

Argus slept in an attic room. He left the next morning, after a big breakfast that put him in good heart for the day. He did not see the old farmer, but his wife farewelled the boy warmly, slipping extra food into his pack as he left the house and strode out towards the road, eager to resume his journey. He walked all day with only a few short stops, and by late afternoon had covered a great distance.

Chapter Three

That evening Argus had his first bout of what he supposed was homesickness. It was not that he wanted to be at home; on the contrary, he was enjoying his freedom and the new world that he was exploring, but he missed the warmth and closeness of family living. He did not connect his sadness with his stay at the farmhouse the previous night, but he did know that he felt unbearably lonely. Not bothering to light a fire, he ate a cold evening meal and rolled up in his blanket, thinking about the way his parents would be spending the evening. To his alarm, he found he could only summon an exact image of their faces when he placed them in familiar situations. He could envisage his father's face clearly when he imagined him winding the great clock that stood in the entrance hallway; and he could see his mother's face when he thought of her studying the night sky and making notes in her voluminous astronomy diaries. For a moment he had an unexpected glimpse of his sister's face too, as he had last seen her, running down to the river, shouting something about Argus getting tea ready. At this memory sadness overwhelmed the boy completely and he wept into his blanket until he fell asleep.

By the next afternoon he was in country so far from

the mountains of his childhood that they could no longer be seen. Instead he was walking through lush and prosperous farmlands, along a well-used road beside a broad river that rolled over the landscape like a lazy carpet. Willows and other trees lined the river's banks. By Argus' standards, the land was densely settled, and encounters with people were frequent. He came to fields lined with wooden frames, upon which green vines grew. Many people of all ages were at work, picking from the vines.

Argus watched from the shadows of the roadside for some minutes before he noticed an artist just a short distance from him: a middle-aged man painting the pastoral scene on a canvas mounted on a large easel. Although the man showed no interest in Argus, the boy approached and stood watching, comparing the painting to the activity in the field. After Argus had sufficient time for a close scrutiny, the man asked rather impatiently, 'Well, what do you think?'

Argus felt a little out of his depth; rather than comment on the artistry of the painting he thought it safer to take a different tack. 'It must be hard,' he said shyly, 'to paint something when it keeps changing all the time.' The man looked at him in apparent surprise, then resumed his work. 'I mean,' said Argus, 'which moment are you painting? This one? Or the last one? Or one from this morning?'

'Yes,' said the man, 'It's always difficult to take something that's moving and full of life and turn it into something that is still. Not even death can do that.'

'What's harder?' asked Argus. 'Taking something moving and freezing it, or taking something three-dimensional and making it flat?'

The man put down his brush and turned to face his

young interrogator. 'You're a remarkable boy,' he said. 'Do you like art?'

'I don't know,' Argus replied. 'I've never seen much. But I like real things better, I think. I mean, I'd rather see a tree than a painting of one. I think it must be frustrating for you, because even if you do a thousand paintings of a tree, it's never going to be as good as the real one.'

'Yes,' said the man. 'It may sound trite, but Nature is the great artist, and we can only imitate her. But supposing a painting gives you a new way of looking at something, so that you get an insight into it that you didn't have before... I mean, a portrait might show you an aspect of someone that you hadn't noticed... a sadness or a sense of joy or a thoughtfulness in the eyes... wouldn't it make the painting worthwhile if it could do that?'

Argus studied the man's landscape again, only this time more closely. He saw the weary way in which the pickers' backs were shown bending over the crops. He saw the careless lines in which the frames had been arranged. And he saw the shadows thrown by the poplars in the afternoon sunlight. 'Why don't I notice these things when I look at the field itself?' he wondered.

Without speaking to the man again Argus walked a little way along the fenceline and stood watching the scene with eyes that were more discerning. He realised that he did not need paintings, just keener eyes. 'He's not only describing what we both see,' he thought. 'He's commenting on it as well. I suppose everyone does that when they paint or tell a story, or dance something, or sing about it...' He recalled his attempts the night before to remember the faces of his family and decided that despite his moment's fear that he would not be able to visualise them, he preferred to carry his own living pictures in his mind rather than rely on 'dead' pictures on canvas. 'My mind's full of millions of pictures,' he thought. 'I just need to know how to look each one up.' He tried to imagine a square cut out of the view in front of him and replaced with a painting of the missing section, and decided that no painting could ever be adequate.

Lost in thought Argus wandered back to the painter, who had stopped work and was taking food from his bag. The boy stood looking at the painting again, admiring the skill with which it was executed. 'Share my lunch with me?' the man asked, offering Argus a piece of pie, which he accepted gratefully. 'You know,' his host continued as they both settled down on the ground with their backs against trees, 'everyone needs some kind of outlet for the artist that's in them. Doesn't matter whether it's painting or writing or carving or music. Everyone's got to have that outlet, and if they don't, they get a kind of madness in them, and there's no sense to be had from them, no sense at all. What about you? What does the artist in you do?'

Argus was taken by surprise and tried to think. 'I suppose my leatherwork,' he said hesitantly. 'I like making belts and stuff like that.' He wondered about his parents, and decided that his mother's astronomy was an outlet for her, but it was more difficult to identify one for his father. Gardening, perhaps? He seemed to get a lot of pleasure from the flowers he grew in his garden.

As the two of them ate under the trees Argus pondered the scene in front of him once more. 'What are they growing?' he asked.

'Grapes,' the man replied, showing no surprise at the question.

'Is there much work around?'

'Yes, they'd probably take you on, but it's not easy.'

'No, I can see that from your painting.' Argus finished his pie and licked the crumbs from his lips, then leaned back, drowsily enjoying the afternoon sun. He could hear the occasional murmur of voices from the pickers, who were gradually moving closer to them. He heard the chattering of the frustrated parrots in the trees on the far side of the field. The rich warm smells of the harvest settled around him as his eyes slowly closed. He said to the artist, 'It's a pity you can't paint smells and sounds and flavours' but the man, who had resumed his painting, did not reply. Or did he say, 'I do'? Argus, asleep from his ears down, could not be sure.

Chapter Four

That evening Argus was caught in a violent thunderstorm that frightened him. He was soaked through. It did not last long, but at its climax a tree on a slight rise on the other side of the river was struck by lightning and exploded with a booming crash. The world was reduced to nothing but noise. Argus knew he was probably not going to be frizzled by a stray bolt, but it was exciting to realise that it was a possibility. He enjoyed the storm while being terrified by it and wishing it would end. When the thunder and lightning finally moved away, across the plains, a heavy downpour of rain completed the drenching of the shivering boy, who by this stage was huddled under a fallen tree. He waited until the showers too had ended and nothing was left of the storm but an unspectacular drizzle; then he set out across the fields for some trees that he guessed concealed and sheltered some buildings.

It was a long and uncomfortable walk but his guess proved to be correct: the trees hid a farm, a large white house, a spread of outbuildings and yards. The house was too grand for Argus, who felt that he was probably a miserable sight in his bedraggled clothes. And there were wet strands of hair plastered across his forehead.

He picked out a large low building on the edge of the complex and slipped over towards it. The smells and scuffling noises emanating from it suggested to him that it was the stables. Argus entered the building quickly and quietly, but there were no people there. The horses, most of whom were eating from feed-bins, paid him no attention. Argus, however, was astounded by their number. He had never seen so many horses in one place in his life. He walked down the central aisle of the building, examining them more closely. They were fine-looking creatures, obviously well-tended, though Argus, a farmer's son, thought rather contemptuously that they would not be good for more than an hour's hard work at a time. He was accustomed to the sturdier, less glamorous mountain ponies.

But the building was dry and warm and the presence of the horses gave it a homely feeling. Argus found an empty stall and stripped off his clothing, then leant over into the adjacent pen and grabbed an old towel that was hanging there, which had obviously been used to rub down the animals. The occupant of the stall, a restless-looking, beautifully-contoured young stallion, tossed his head and glared at the boy.

'Don't worry,' said Argus, grinning to himself, 'I won't be bending over in front of you.' The stallion pranced a little, then went back to his food. Argus began to dry himself, wondering if he had ever experienced anything so good as the feeling of the rough, worn towel on his damp body. He felt the blood sing under his skin once more. He completed the job by drying his hair, not knowing or caring that he was making it stick up like the hay under his feet. He put the towel back on its nail and stood looking down at himself, taking pleasure in the evidence of the long-awaited growth that his body was now indisputably experiencing. He had never been taught about sex in his life, but his years on the farm left him in no doubt or confusion about what was happening to him. He looked at the stallion again. 'Not up to your standards, maybe,' he said to the horse, who had now lost interest in him, 'but good enough for me.'

He began to finger himself curiously; the object of his interest, already stimulated by the attention he had been paying it, quickly rose to full arousal. Argus continued to touch it, lightly and smoothly, as irresistible feelings grew in him and his hand moved more urgently. There was no gainsaying the feelings: Argus realised that he would be compelled to go on until his body gave him permission to stop. The pleasure was becoming so great as to be almost frightening, and it was obvious to the boy that this time, unlike his earlier immature adventurings, there would be a definite climax, not just the inconclusive excitement he had enjoyed in the past. He continued to stroke himself, fascinated by the growing thickness and coarseness of his organ, by its darkening colour, until at last the inevitable happened, and he was grabbing at himself and at the unbearably stiff thing that had temporarily become the centre and focus of his life, and which was now convulsively shooting jets of thin liquid across the hay.

For a few moments Argus stood in the stall, bent over, exhausted by the intensity of the experience. Yet he was pleased and proud too, and aware that it was an experience that he would repeat — and perhaps he could enhance it too, he thought, as he imagined a girl's hand doing to him what he had just done to himself. That idea caused him so much turmoil that he had to place it aside; instead he watched with interest the steady detumescence of his penis. He realised that something else had changed: the desire that would plague him for hours in the past had suddenly become a finite thing and had disappeared with the ejaculation of the fluid from his body.

He dressed slowly and walked back down the centre aisle to the store-room that housed the huge feed-bins for the horses. There he made himself a gruel of oats and barley, a meal that he was pleased to flavour with carrots and apples from trays that stood beside the bins. But his greatest delight came when he found a supply of sugar cubes. Starved of sugar since leaving home, he added handfuls of it to his gruel until it was a sweet and syrupy concoction.

Up until then Argus had been acting with complete disregard for the possibility that someone might come into the stables, but after finishing his meal he decided that it was time to take a little care. He eventually settled in a row of unoccupied stalls at the back of the building, choosing the second last one as his bed for the night. He knew from his experience at home that hay was not comfortable unless a good covering was available, so he used his own blanket as well as a couple of horse rugs from the tack-room. Sometime quite late into the night he heard voices and could see a reflection of a moving light dancing along the ceiling: another horse was being brought in and stabled, after a journey perhaps, but the activity was well away from Argus' corner and the boy soon went back to sleep.

Chapter Five

For the first time on his journey Argus found that he was never out of sight of buildings and, by inference, people. He was constantly passing cottages, guesthouses and farmhouses. Occasionally he went by a cluster of buildings that could be called a hamlet. He enjoyed the evidence of increasing life that was all around him; he gazed curiously at each new sight and approached each bend in the road with anticipation. There were new problems for him — mainly the difficulty of finding places to sleep — but there were compensations too, particularly the plentiful food supplies. Many of the fields he passed were given over to market gardens, and after dark these provided him with a varied diet.

He worked for a few days in an orchard, picking oranges for a married couple who spoke neither to each other nor to him. Their moroseness did not bother Argus, but the work did. It was hot and boring and dirty. As he flicked each orange towards him to be picked, the accumulated layer of dirt on top of the fruit flew into his face; by the end of each day he was spectacularly black. Still, the food was good, and he supplemented the meals by eating huge numbers of oranges, despite the obvious irritation this caused his employers. After four days they told him they would not be needing him any more. As there were still plenty of oranges to be picked, he could only assume that they were not satisfied with his work. Certainly he had been quite slow, but he swung his pack onto his back and set off again without great concern. He did, however, take a dozen oranges with him; they weighed a lot but the refreshment they gave was sweet and nourishing.

As he walked on he quickened his pace, knowing from signs on the road, and from conversations with other travellers, that he was closing in on the large town of Ifeka. The curiosity and excitement that had been sparking in him for a long time now burned steadily. He had never seen a town bigger than Random. Now he was walking past rows of houses that were close together. Children played in their gardens, and there were footpaths made of gravel beside well-defined roads. Sometimes stretches of countryside broke up the clusters of houses, but gradually these became less and less frequent. He slept that night in a haystack, guessing that it could be his last such bed for quite a time. Next morning he was off early, after an oddly mixed breakfast of carrots and oranges.

The traffic became quite heavy and Argus had to adjust his pace occasionally when held up behind family groups or older people. He did not mind but was surprised to find that for the first time on his journey people were not meeting his eye and smiling or exchanging friendly words. He passed a man working in his flower garden. Argus gave him a cordial greeting and stopped to chat, as was the custom in his own valley, but the man ignored him and kept stolidly pulling up weeds. Argus, disconcerted, did not know what to do. He waited for a long, embarrassed moment and finally went on his way, but his cheeks burned for a long time at the insult.

Around lunchtime Argus noticed crowds of people and a number of large tents on a rather poorly maintained common a few hundred yards from the road. Filled with curiosity he went over and mingled with the crowd. It appeared that he had stumbled across some kind of fair, or travelling show. There were food stalls, games, a dance troupe, storytellers, and displays of various oddities, some of them animate and some definitely inanimate. The latter included a collection of carvings made from human bones, and a rock said to have come from the moon. The animate were not so easily visible: there were pictures of them outside a tent but to see them in the flesh, one had to pay. They were supposed to include a two-headed woman, a fat lady, a human skeleton and a person who was half man-half woman. Argus could not pay his money quickly enough, and, heart fluttering with excitement, he went in.

The inside of the tent was shadowy and it took his eyes a few moments to adjust. The exhibits were arranged in a circle of small booths. Other spectators were walking around examining the displays and at each booth there was a low murmur of conversation. Argus went across to the nearest stand and found himself gazing into the eyes of a man of incredible thinness, who was seated on a stool and looking at the spectators. He wore a long tall top hat, and it, like the rest of his strange garb, was striped in orange and green, colours which accentuated his remarkable shape. Argus felt he could have joined his thumb and forefinger around the man's arms or legs, without any trouble at all. He was reminded of a praying mantis, and giggled at the thought, then blushed at his rudeness. There were people beside him who were not so sensitive, however.

'Hey mister,' a girl called out, 'can I take you home? We need a new scarecrow.' The crowd tittered but the man continued to look blandly into their faces. 'Guess he's heard every line before,' Argus thought, moving on to the next stall. There was a bigger crowd here, watching what Argus supposed was the two-headed woman. In fact the two-headed woman was two girls who were joined at the stomach. They were seated half facing each other, in the only possible position they could have adopted, and were playing cards, ignoring their fascinated audience. Occasionally one would speak to the other but only in monosyllables, and only to comment on the card game. Argus, not as self-conscious here as he had been with the living skeleton, whose direct gaze he had found disconcerting, stayed a long time, until one of the girls, in the middle of shuffling the cards, looked at him with a casual grin and said, 'Hiya honey, you live round here?'

Argus gulped and shook his head, then found his tongue and said, 'No, in the Random valley.'

'Well, that's quite a way off,' the girl said, and Argus warmed to her as someone among all these strangers who appeared to know his home district. The other girl, however, gave him a sour glance and picked up her cards without a comment.

Argus waited a while but the twins said nothing more to him, so he moved on. The fat lady, astoundingly fat, wobbling all over every time she moved or laughed, was deep in conversation with one of the spectators, while she knitted a long scarf. Argus listened to them talking; it was mainly about the fair. It seemed to be a nomadic life, travelling to another town every week or two, always on the road. The longer the fat lady talked, the more ordinary she seemed to Argus, just like some of the women from Random. The boy left her and crossed to another booth, this time the half man-half woman display.

Here was a person who was groomed and dressed as though split down the middle. One half was male: a short haircut, a moustache, men's clothing. But all that ceased at the dividing line: the moustache was only half a moustache, the clothing specially designed. The hair on the female side was long and decorated with beads. The group gazing at this person was the biggest and quietest group of all. Argus stood at the side and watched with them, fascinated but anxious to avoid notice. There was something frightening yet compelling about the quiet figure who was looking out into the distance, over the heads of the crowd. Argus shivered and walked away. In front of him, as he left the tent, was a group of young people. They were subdued until they got out into the bright sunshine but then they broke into an uproar of speculation and jokes about the hermaphroditic figure they had left behind.

Argus bought some stuffed capsicums for lunch then wandered among the various shows and games. He sat on the grass and listened to a balladeer with a piano accordion, who was singing a melancholy song about a shipwreck. Finally growing bored with the entertainment, he strolled a little further afield, into what was clearly the living area for the members of the travelling fair. It was a quiet part of the common, spread with caravans and tents; few people, apart from toddlers, were to be seen.

Outside one caravan, however, was a man with a brown

beard, who was tying pieces of fishing line together. Around him, all over the ground, was a scatter of bits and pieces of fishing equipment. As Argus approached, the man said, with barely a glance at him, 'Here, give me a hand will you. Put your thumb there, while I tie this.'

'What kind of knot are you tying?' asked Argus, obliging but rather sceptical about the ugly lump the man was producing in his line.

'I don't know,' the man said with a laugh. 'I don't know much about fishing and I don't know much about knots. This is my grandfather's stuff. No-one's used it since he died, so I thought I'd better have a go at it.'

'I think you should be using a blood knot,' said Argus with authority.

The man looked up at him, this time with real interest. 'Well, go right ahead' he said, promptly handing the whole mess over to the boy.

Argus went to work, quickly tying the difficult knot to connect the first two thick pieces, but labouring some-what as the pieces became thinner and his hands and eyes became tired. For the twenty minutes or so that it took Argus to do the job, the man watched quietly, helping where he could but generally proving too clumsy to be of real use.

'You're a country boy, I'll be bound?' he asked Argus when the task was at last completed. 'Yes,' Argus nodded, 'from near Random.'

'Yes, I thought so. These town boys have a different air about them. What are you doing in these parts?'

'Oh, just wandering,' Argus said vaguely, still mindful that he was not supposed to discuss his quest.

'Ah, I see,' the man said. 'I'm sorry I asked. It's just

that one forgets... the old customs. I guess your folk
live in the traditional way. We've been travelling in the
populated areas too long. Once there was a time when
many a lad like you could be seen following his star across
the countryside. Yes, and girls too. Guess it just became
too dangerous for many.'

There was a pause while Argus digested all this. 'What
do you do with the fair?' he asked then.

'I'm a storyteller,' the man replied.

Argus, who had a great love for stories, warmed to
him immediately. 'My name's Argus,' he said.

'I'm Mayon,' the storyteller responded, and the two
gravely shook hands. Knowing that the time would come
when he would have to be a storyteller himself, seven times
over, Argus wondered what he could learn from this man.
The opportunity came unexpectedly when Mayon said,
'Why don't you get a job here for a while?'

'Could I?' Argus asked in surprise.

'Oh yes, no great problem. They always prefer to take
on country boys. And there's not a week goes by that
someone doesn't leave; so if there's no vacancy today, there
will be tomorrow, in a manner of speaking. These shows
always attract drifters. Any strong lad with a practical
mind and a good pair of hands can walk into a job here
pretty easily. If you're interested I'll send you over to my
brother's caravan. He's in charge of the stringers — they're
the, you know, workers. The fellows who put the tents
up and so on.'

Within twenty minutes, to Argus' great pleasure, he was
hired as a stringer by Jud, Mayon's brother. He was given
a bed and a cupboard in Mayon's caravan, and sent off
on his first job — to pick up litter around the shows

where he had so recently been an interested customer and spectator.

He worked on various odd jobs until well into the night, with only a brief break when he was invited to dip into Mayon's cooking pot and serve himself a generous helping of a concoction in which mushrooms, carrots, tomatoes and herbs figured prominently. He was grateful when he was at last free, at around midnight, and he could fall into bed and sleep. It was the first late night he had had since leaving home; and it was the noisiest and most crowded evening that he had ever spent. He had become used to nights spent in solitude under the stars, reviewing the day's events and thinking his own thoughts. But tonight sleep was upon him too quickly to allow for any conscious thinking.

Chapter Six

As Argus gradually learnt the routines of life with the folk at the fair he was able to do his work more and more automatically, which allowed him time to get to know his surroundings from the inside. His duties were menial — cleaning, painting, repairing, carrying, general labouring. For quite a time though hardly anyone except Mayon and a couple of other stringers spoke to him, even to give him a 'good morning'. 'Be patient,' Mayon advised. 'They're used to stringers coming and going every week or two, like I told you. They get sick of being friendly with someone who leaves the next day.' So Argus took particular trouble to do his jobs well and to be polite to everyone, and soon he was pleased to see that the thaw forecast by Mayon was taking place.

As he got to know his new companions better he met with many surprises. The fat lady, whose name was Ruth, was the easiest — besides Mayon — to befriend. She was naturally gregarious, spending all her spare time sitting in the sun at the front of her caravan, collecting gossip and chatting with all who passed. She could not walk far without suffering loss of breath and overheating, so she found it easier to avoid exertion. But Argus could not understand why she was as fat as she was; for she did not seem to eat a lot. Yet she was so fat that if she sat on a chair it would immediately sink into the ground up to its cross-bars, and indeed all her own furniture had been specially made to accommodate her. 'And my mother was such a little thing' she confided wheezingly to Argus. 'Why, if I sneezed she'd be blown across the room. And I was so tiny when I was born.' She laughed uproariously, and her great sides shook as though she were an ocean in a storm. 'Now my ears alone would weigh what I did at birth.'

The conjoined twins, Lavolta and Parara, held a great fascination for Argus. He found that Parara, who had spoken to him that first day in the tent, was quite different from her sister. Parara was lively, humorous and outgoing, while her sister was dour and elusive. Parara would greet everyone she knew with warmth and pleasure, and stop to chat. Lavolta, who obviously had no choice then but to stop too, would stand slightly turned away, gazing into the distance and contributing little or nothing to the conversation. One day when Argus asked the twins to help him for a moment, by keeping the tension on a coil of rope he was unwinding to fence off a new enclosure, it was Parara who took the rope and did all the work.

The twins moved around with as much speed and facility as any single person, even though their gait was awkward and graceless. They appeared to have harmonised most of their living relationships; Argus never witnessed an argument between them about when they should eat, for example, or when they should go to bed. Like everyone else he wondered about their visits to the toilet, or what happened if one of the girls had a boyfriend, but he was never brave enough or rude enough to ask. The twins were able to laugh at themselves, but Argus knew they were often asked coarse questions by the crowds who came through the main tent to look at them. He did not want to place himself on that level.

A more disturbing figure was that of Tiresias, the shadowy half man-half woman whom Argus had found so unsettling when he first laid eyes on him. Argus could not decide to which sex he belonged. Under the artificial embellishments of the special clothes, the moustache, and the haircut, Tiresias was truly a sexually ambiguous figure. And he did not make it any easier for Argus to satisfy his curiosity, because he was always elusive. Seldom seen around the campsite, he kept mainly to his caravan, where, Jud claimed, he made a fortune by entertaining local men in search of something exotic. When all the members of the travelling show were gathered around the big bonfire late at night, as was their custom, Tiresias could sometimes be seen standing unobtrusively in the background, well away from the bright firelight. Argus spoke to him occasionally and was always given a polite answer, expressed in a toneless yet pleasant enough voice that was also sexually indefinable. Argus was unable to explain the fascination and fear that he felt towards Tiresias, but a prickling on the back of his neck and a reddening of his skin always told him when he was near the mysterious half man-half woman.

Another of the exotic figures who had attracted Argus' attention on his first walk through the big show tent was Titius, the human skeleton. This tall and spindly fellow proved, however, to be boring and irritating. He hung around listlessly all day when not 'on duty', complaining to anyone who would listen about anything that was currently annoying him. His fretting wore out Argus' patience and the boy soon learned to avoid him.

It was the storytellers and the balladeers to whom Argus was most attracted though. As well as Mayon, there were two other storytellers: Delta and Cassim, both women, and two balladeers: Cameron and Demy. Whenever they gave public performances Argus tried to arrange his jobs so that he could be nearby; and late at night, when work was over and everyone relaxed, Argus loved to listen to them talk and sing. He particularly liked the fact that they so rarely told the same story twice, or that when they did, they gave it enough new twists to retain its interest. But on the other hand, there were songs whose very familiarity accounted for their attraction, and which he never tired of hearing.

One night Demy sang a ballad which Argus had not heard before but which he was never to forget. There were only a few people left around the fire when Demy picked up his guitar and began:

> Now let me sing you a story
> Of a child who died one sad day.
> It's a song of love and of loyalty
> And the price a girl had to pay.
>
> Eleven years old, she went walking
> Down the bed of a stream
> And she walked through the water so carefree
> Lost in her own private dream.
>
> The name of the girl was Sunday
> And she lived up Random way.

She had a dog called Milo
Who was walking with her that day.

Milo was leaping through water,
Loving the splash and the spray,
Staying ahead of his mistress,
The beautiful girl, Sunday.

The dog found a cliff where the water
Fell a hundred feet sheer
And he stood on the edge looking over
With not a tremor of fear.

But Sunday, she saw the danger.
She knew of the boulders below.
She started forward to save him,
To save the dog Milo.

The rocks were wet with the water
And sleek with the moss so green,
The dog turned and slipped, as his mistress
Slid on the bright stony sheen.

The two went over together,
Embraced in love and in fear.
The boulders stood waiting to break them,
To become their funeral bier.

And their bodies lay fatally shattered
On the rocks at the foot of the fall.

But the girl so true and so faithful,
She was not broken at all.
No, the girl so true and so faithful,
She was not broken at all.

Demy finished the song with a sad chord and sat looking
into the fire, his head bowed. Since the mention of Random
and the name Sunday Argus had been frozen with fear
and horror. But Mayon turned to him and said, 'You're
from Random aren't you? Does the story ring a bell with
you?' Then he saw from the tears on Argus' face that
it did indeed.

'No-one knows,' said Argus, his voice breaking with
long-suppressed sobs, 'no-one knows if that's the way it
really happened. But we think that's probably right.' He
wiped his face and stood up. 'How did you come to hear
of her?' he asked Demy.

'I was in the valley at the time' the man answered,
embarrassed at the grief he had caused the boy. 'Everyone
was talking about it. The people were devastated. She
seemed to be such a loved child. I wrote the song a few
weeks later, after I'd moved on to other parts. I was a
wandering balladeer at the time, travelling on my own.'

'Everyone did love her,' Argus sobbed, tears running
down his face again. 'When you're a kid, you don't think
that you love your sister exactly, but you know that you
care about her and you'd rather die yourself than have
any harm come to her. But it's not enough to want to
save someone. Now I know I love her but I can't tell
her that, and I miss her. I miss her all the time.' He stumbled
away into the darkness, out into the empty expanse of
the common, but Mayon came after him and led him

gently to a rock where they could both sit. 'I'm sorry about crying back there,' the boy said, 'in front of everyone.'

'Tears are part of the healing,' Mayon answered. 'They're one of the ways your soul heals itself after a wound. Just like when you're hot your body sweats, to bring your temperature down.'

'But I still don't understand why people have to die,' Argus said. 'I guess that's one of the things I'm meant to have worked out before I go home again, but some of the questions just seem too hard sometimes.'

'Nothing dies,' Mayon answered him. 'There is no death. Just change. Nature understands that. It's only Man who doesn't. Death is an invention of Man. Your sister's body is metamorphosing back into the rich earth in which she is buried. Her atoms are rearranging into new and wonderful patterns. A flower gets eaten by an insect; it changes into part of the body of that insect. The insect is eaten by a trout; it becomes part of that trout. The trout gets old and stops breathing; its poor body disintegrates and gets washed away until it reintegrates with the soil and humus, along the fertile river flats. And from that soil grows a flower once more. That's what happens to our physical bodies in the process called death.

Your sister was more than just a body. A head and a trunk and four limbs. Do you think that's all you are? No. That's not you. There's much more to you. Inside that arrangement of flesh and bones there's an abstract, indefinable something that is the real you and is a collage of your past and present, all the experiences and feelings and thoughts that you've ever had. And when the time comes for that essential you to leave its physical body, then away it goes, on fresh adventures, into a state of being that we can be sure will provide us with more new and wonderful experiences, even if we can be sure of nothing else about it.'

The man and the boy were silent, looking out into the mysterious darkness. 'I can never understand why people get buried in those big solid coffins,' Mayon said at last. 'It just interferes with the process of change. Makes it hard for the physical body to move on to its next stage.' The two stood and walked slowly back to the bonfire, whose flames had now become coals and would soon be ashes.

'I'm glad Demy wrote the song,' Argus said. 'It's nice to know she's remembered like that.' Presently they retired to the caravan, for the healing process called sleep. Argus had not shared a bed with anyone since, as a little boy afraid of storms, he had snuggled in with his sister, but this night he climbed in under Mayon's eiderdown and, comforted by the gentle storyteller's warmth, he spent the night at peace.

Chapter Seven

Two days later, knowing that the show was about to pack its tents and vans and move to a new town, Argus resolved to explore Ifeka while he still had a chance. For all the time he had spent there he had only seen the outer suburbs. He received permission from Jud to take a day off and go into the centre of town.

He went with a light heart and high expectations. It took him just forty minutes walking before he found himself, for the first time in his life, in busy market streets where he had to wend his way through masses of people and where it was hard to see more than a few yards ahead. Argus was excited by the pressing crowds, the smells, the constant noise, the frenetic hurry that seemed to infect the very paving stones of the roads. No-one seemed to notice anyone else; everyone was absorbed in his or her own affairs. There were a few exceptions though: a merry woman with laughing eyes helped Argus pick up some coins that he dropped as he fumbled for change; and an old woman suddenly remarked to the boy, as they stood waiting for a break in the traffic, 'You know, I saw a daffodil growing through the cracks in the pavement here once'. Argus was too surprised to be able to think of an answer; before he could do anything more than smile politely the lady had seized her opportunity to join the throng, and was gone.

In a slightly quieter street on the edge of the main market area Argus settled himself into an aperture between two stone buildings, to watch the panorama of life in Ifeka. His main interest was the stall-holders, rather than the customers, as they, absorbed in their shopping, were a less colourful lot. The merchants seemed casually in control of the pavement. They chattered and laughed and visited each other, and enjoyed shared jokes.

As Argus watched, their personalities became more apparent. A huge man selling cheese dominated the street. Flushed and jovial, he was more involved in conversation than in business, and seemed almost to resent interruptions from customers wishing to buy. He was constantly laughing and rubbing his hands with pleasure, the gregarious centre of attention in the alley-way. Although Argus enjoyed his larger-than-life egotism, it occurred to him that the other stall-holders might dislike the man's power, under which thin men chafed and muttered. Argus was reminded of Hammond, a young farmer from his own valley, who similarly dominated others by the sheer strength of his personality. He was popular, but resented.

The boy looked at the other traders, seeking proof of his theory about the cheese-seller. Occasionally they responded to the big man's cannoning comments, but they turned away from him at the end of their terse responses, sometimes grinning in complicity at a neighbour. Argus was starting to feel satisfied that he was right when suddenly his theory was thrown off-balance, and he was forced to wonder if the man was not a genial buffoon instead.

A woman from an adjoining stall called out, 'Come on Grobian, business is too slack. Get a few customers for us.' Her good-humoured cry was echoed by others, and Grobian, after a little show of reluctance, took off his apron and came out into the middle of the lane, where he placed his hat on the ground and began a comic dance, strutting around the hat and singing:

> I'm a big brown teddy bear,
> Stuffed with cotton wool and air.
> I've got eyes, left and right,
> Peeping from my skin so tight.
> My claws are big and sharp and strong,
> They take me where I don't belong.
> If you want a new bear rug
> I'll give you a big BEAR HUG.

On the last two words Grobian rushed at a woman in the crowd. As she shrieked and laughed he picked her up in a huge embrace. Then, putting her down and taking a handful of eggs from his stall, he began juggling the eggs and singing a song about cheese. Argus could only wonder at the many dimensions of this man and, he supposed, of all men and women. He recalled the warning in his father's old leather book that he had read, so long ago it seemed now: the warning that nothing was simple, that all things were complex, including people.

By the end of his show Grobian had gathered quite a crowd into the street. The big man was flushed with the success and exhilaration that can only come from public performance. He lingered in the middle of the alley, talking to a few onlookers who had not strayed away again to look at the merchandise. He even ignored two customers who were waiting to buy cheese.

Argus came out of his niche, wandered down the street and turned the corner into a broader thoroughfare. Here a vendor was selling ice cream. Argus watched as people bought the cones and walked away licking them with every evidence of pleasure. Though he had never tasted this food before, the boy purchased a cone and gingerly applied his tongue to the white mound. The coldness startled him and numbed his tongue. He jerked his head back and held the ice cream at a distance, studying it with amused perplexity; then, realising that some children were giggling at him, he turned away and continued down the street, taking experimental licks as he went. Once he had become accustomed to the shock of the coldness, he decided that he liked the taste very much indeed. But he chose, with typical conservatism, to make the pleasure last as long as possible. Having eaten half the ice cream, he put the rest in his pocket to enjoy later, and tried to ignore the coldness that seeped through his clothing to the skin of his leg.

As Argus came to the next corner, a woman, walking quickly, drew level with him; then, after a slight pause, she turned left and hurried down a narrow lane. A moment later a man also overtook him and followed the route that the woman had taken. Argus instinctively sensed tension in the speed of the two walkers and in the rapidly shrinking distance between them. He followed, as the woman came to the end of the lane and hesitated at the stream of traffic passing in front of her. At that moment the man caught up and placed his hand on her shoulder. The woman started like a half-wild horse at the contact,

49

and said something to the man that Argus could not hear. He heard the man's rejoinder though: 'You're coming back', and he understood the tone of the message.

Forgetting courtesy, he watched open-mouthed as the man grabbed at the woman's arm and pulled her roughly. Argus thought he should intervene, but the man looked much too big and strong for him; and besides, he wondered if this was perhaps the normal way of things in the city. Then an old woman arrived huffing and creaking.

'What are you doing, Tira?' she said crossly to the girl. 'Causing such a scene. You ought to be ashamed.'

'You don't know what he's like,' the younger woman answered angrily.

'As bad as you, that's what he's like. You're well suited.' The three of them started walking back along the alley, accusations and counter-accusations flying between them. Argus watched spellbound till they were out of sight.

Just as they turned the corner and disappeared from his view the boy became aware of a trickle down his leg. He looked, and saw a white runnel of forgotten ice cream; at the same time he felt again the chilled wet patch from his pocket. Not knowing the ways of ice cream, the boy was astounded. But his attempts to remove the half-melted mess from his pocket were a disaster. He hated to throw any away, so he tried licking it off his hands, which quickly became a sticky embarrassment. And no matter how much he tried to clean out his pocket it seemed impossible — a cold Augean dip. It was not until he found a drinking-fountain, twenty minutes later, that he was able to clean himself properly and bid farewell to his first ice cream.

For the rest of the afternoon Argus roamed the streets and enjoyed the sights of the town. He saw a dog being wheeled along on a large red trolley by an old man who was apparently its owner. He saw a stall full of enormous orchids and was as staggered by their blatant beauty as he was frightened by their fierce mouths. He saw a caged bird singing a song that Argus knew was one of despair. And he saw other sights that he did not understand: a clock with numbers in the wrong sequence, a woman walking quickly along the street talking to herself, a man dressed in wedding clothes standing alone on a street corner.

As he passed one building Argus was accosted by a middle-aged woman with dark hair and a golden collar around her neck. 'I know what you're doing,' she said to the boy. 'And you'll find part of it in here. There are a lot of answers in this house.' She put her arm on his shoulder, in a familiar but over-intimate gesture. 'Come on in,' she said. 'Have you got some money? It won't cost much. And you'll have a good time. Don't you want to be a man?'

Argus instinctively shied away from her touch. 'No, no,' he stammered, unsure of what he was being offered but unable to trust the woman. 'I'm in a hurry.' He started to move away but the woman tried to detain him.

'Oh, come on,' she said. 'Don't be frightened. It'll be the best afternoon of your life.'

When the boy kept backing away the woman lost interest in him and he was able to make good his departure. Yet he felt humiliated by the encounter: it made him feel smaller and younger than he believed himself to be.

A few blocks further on Argus came to a high wire fence which seemed to separate one part of the town from the other. Try as he might, he could find no break in this fence, and eventually he was forced to abandon his search. He stood for quite a time looking through the mesh. In the distance he could see figures moving, people going about their business in, apparently, much the same way as the people on his side. Yet none of them came close enough to the fence for him to speak to them; so the function of the barrier remained a mystery.

It was getting late in the afternoon and Argus realised it was time to start back for the fair. Suddenly he felt such a rush of weariness that he doubted whether he had the strength to walk all that way. Yet he knew he had no choice, and he forced himself to call up reserves from the bottomless pit of energy that had never failed him in the past. With a determined lifting of the head he began walking.

The stalls were closing as he passed through the market areas once more. From one that was still open he purchased some food; it appeared to be a mixture of cheese and fruit, wrapped in unleavened bread. It was delicious and he ate it hungrily. It freshened his body somehow, and after that he found the walk easier.

On the edge of the market area he recognised a House of the Past. He had not been in one since Random but he entered it with gratitude, and sat in its peace for half an hour or so, before resuming the journey to the common in the quickening dark of twilight.

The event of the day that gave him the greatest pleasure, however, was the warm welcome he received from Mayon and Jud and Demy and Parara and others who were cooking around the main fire when he returned.

'Here's the farm boy, back from the big city,' gurgled Ruth, the friendly fat woman. 'Find any cows to milk dear? Seen all the sights? Here, sit down next to me and have a bowl of soup and tell me about all the temptations you gave in to.' Argus knew he was back among friends and his heart warmed to them. When the fair moved, the day after next, he went with them.

Chapter Eight

On the first night after the company left Ifeka they camped on a low windswept plain near a small lake. There was a strange tang in the air, a taste on the wind, that Mayon told Argus was the first sharp bite of the ocean. Argus was excited and enchanted. He sat late that night at the big fire, enjoying the cold salt ruffles of air on his face, until the only people left around the coals were Ruth, Mayon, the male-female Tiresias, the storytellers Delta and Cassim, the spidery Titius and a dark, attractive young girl named Temora, who had been employed as a stringer just before the convoy left Ifeka.

Argus was only half listening to the conversation, which was about the town of Wintle, where they were headed. With zest and good humour, Ruth was recounting the story of her last trip to Wintle, when she had apparently married a man who had deserted her a week later. Argus did not know how much, if any, of the story was true, but it did not seem to matter to anyone else. 'A good story is a good story' was the creed of the professional storytellers of the fair, and Argus was inclined to agree with them.

'It was a wonderful honeymoon,' Ruth sighed romantically, 'until we had an argument one night over who should put the cat out. Well, you know how hard it is for me to get up at nights. Every other night he put it out, but this night he dug his little heels in and nothing would shift him. Maybe I'd worn him out.' She gave a throaty chuckle. 'So there was nothing else for it but for me to get up and do it myself. Oh, I wasn't half mad. So after I'd put the cat out I came back and put him out too. He kicked and struggled but I wasn't having any. I threw him out the door, down the steps, and that was it. After I'd closed the door on him I never saw him again.'

'Yes, I remember,' said Cassim. 'He was only wearing a pair of shorts. Jud took pity on him and gave him a bed for the night but he went early the next morning, taking Jud's only good set of clothes. And that was the last any of us ever saw of him.'

'Well, he could have been worse off,' Ruth sighed. 'Remember Marma, the fat lady who used to work on the east coast years ago? Did you ever hear what became of her and her man?'

'No, what happened?' Mayon asked.

'Well, she passed out as they were going up a set of stairs one day in the house that they'd bought for their old age. And she fell back on top of the little fellow and crushed him to death. She came to an hour later and found him dead underneath her.'

None of the company seemed to be much moved by this sad tale, except the new girl, Temora. 'It must be hard being a fat lady,' she said quietly.

'Well,' said Ruth, delighted at finding a sympathetic ear, 'it's hard when you have to walk any distance, especially if it's uphill. There's no gainsaying that. And it's not nice when people make unkind remarks to you, like they do in the tent sometimes. But most people just enjoy a chat. I'd have to say, all things considered, that it's been a good life. You see, I've been especially blessed.'

'How's that?' asked Temora.

'Well, you see dear, being a lusus, it means you're given a very fortunate life.'

'What's a lusus?' Argus whispered to Mayon.

'A kind of a freak,' the man whispered back.

But Temora was pursuing the point. 'How do you figure that, fortunate?' she asked. 'I mean, no offence, but I guess most people think if you're born a lusus you've been given a pretty tough deal.'

'Oh no,' the fat woman remonstrated as though the idea had never occurred to her before. 'Oh no, quite the opposite. I mean, everyone's a freak anyway. I'm just lucky that I don't have to work at it. I make a good living out of being myself. I don't have to do anything; people pay to see me as I am, whereas other people have to go and dig potatoes or trade or fish or sew clothes in order to keep themselves alive. They're unlucky that their freakishness just isn't as obvious as mine, so they can't make much of it. Then there's the ones who worry that people can't tell that they're a lusus, so they set out to make themselves a bit more conspicuous. They don't believe people can see it when it's on the inside of them, so they recreate it on the outside, just to be sure. They're the ones who dress funny or paint their bodies or mark themselves. Do you know, I knew a man once, he had messages carved into his skin, all over his body, whole sentences, so you could read him like you'd read a book.'

'What did they say?' asked Mayon with interest.

'Oh, all sorts of things,' Ruth chuckled. 'I remember up his left leg it said: "We always go too far."' She shook with helpless mirth. 'Now ain't that the truth! It's always the simplest words are the truest.' She became serious again. 'But you know, all he was trying to do was to let people know he was a lusus. As if everyone doesn't know that about everyone else already!'

'How do you mean, everyone is?' Argus asked shyly.

'Oh my dear,' the fat lady said. 'We're all different, aren't we? So we're all freaks to each other. Now you look at Mayon here. The way his eyebrows meet in the middle like that. And have you ever noticed his hands? His little finger's as long as his fourth finger.' Mayon gravely held his hands out for inspection, while Ruth continued. 'There ain't a person been born that you can't find something like that about them. But it's not just on the outside, it's on the inside too. Take the other day, when Mayon was reading his book by candlelight, and he got too close to the candle and the book caught on fire — why, everyone else was running around looking for a bucket full of water, and Mayon, what was he doing? Sitting there laughing, that's what.

'And another thing, you watch him when he's about to start eating. He closes his eyes for a minute and says something — very quietly, so that no-one notices but me. And you ask him what he thinks about burials, and what he wants done with his body after he dies. You see, he's got different reactions and thoughts and opinions from everyone else, and so have we all, and that's another way we're all freaks.'

'My nose has got a big bump in the middle,' said Argus. 'And I've got a birthmark on my right leg.'

'Course you have dear,' said Ruth. 'It's all a matter of degree. With me, my fat's more obvious, and on a bigger scale than the bump in your nose, that's all. Now imagine if that bump was the size of a coconut. Why, you'd be able to have my kind of life then, and very lucky you'd think yourself too.'

'I don't think I'm lucky,' said Tiresias, speaking for the first time. He was sitting in the shadows, and Argus could only just make out his slight, ambiguous figure.

'No, well dearie, that's because you accept other people's judgements about you, instead of making up your own mind. You've got to look at yourself from your point of view, not someone else's, and decide for yourself what your good points are, and then what you don't like, and want to change. It's no good being unhappy because other people say you should be. Just like it's no good being happy when everyone tells you how well off you are. The things they think you should feel good or bad about mightn't be the things that mean much to you. People tell you to listen to the song of the thrush, when in your heart you know yours is the song of the night owl. You've got to find your own music. It's already playing inside you; all you have to do is listen a little harder, so it's not drowned out by all the noise around about.'

The last of the coals were still glowing and putting out a surprising amount of warmth. Assisted by Cassim and Mayon, Ruth got to her feet and, with farewells to all, lumbered away to bed. The others too began to leave. Argus and the young girl Temora were left to put out the fire, but they hesitated to do it, so settled was its glow.

'I like Ruth,' Temora said at last. 'She's so kind.'

'Yes,' Argus agreed, 'after a while you forget that she's

fat, and you just think of her as a nice, friendly lady.'

'Isn't it good the way that happens?' Temora said. 'It's the same with the twins. Already I forget that they're connected — they seem such different personalities. But it usually takes longer to get over your first impressions.'

'It works in a sort of opposite way too,' Argus said very nervously, driven to take risks by his growing liking for this dark-haired girl. 'When I first saw you, I thought you were really attractive looking, and I still think so, but that's only on the outside. Until I know you better I won't know what you're like on the inside — what you're really like. It's the opposite but the same, because with the freaks who work here you have to get over your first negative impression, which stops you from seeing them as people; and with someone who's very good-looking, you have to get over your first positive impression, which still stops you from seeing her as a person.'

'Yes, exactly,' Temora said. 'I hate it when people comment on my looks, because I know they're saying nothing at all about me. Absolutely nothing.'

The two sat in silence for a few minutes, not an uncomfortable silence, but one rich with the promise of future possibilities. Finally, however, Temora yawned and stretched. 'I'm going to bed,' she said. 'Do you want me to put out the fire, or are you staying up?'

'I'll stay up,' Argus answered. He sat gazing into the coals for another half an hour, as though he would find the answers to all questions there.

Chapter Nine

The convoy of wagons and caravans moved slowly, at the pace of its slowest member, so that it took two more days to reach the coast. Argus was impatient, yet he passed the time profitably enough. Mayon taught him how to juggle and Parara, the more extroverted of the conjoined twins, told him many stories of their lives in sideshows and fairs. Lavolta interjected occasional comments, usually sour ones, and Argus came to realise that the taunts and blows they suffered had deeply wounded one twin while leaving the other virtually unscathed.

The land was becoming flatter, the ground sandier and the breeze saltier. On their third day out from Ifeka they pitched camp at about four in the afternoon, in a sheltered spot that Mayon said was as close to the sea as they would be for a while. Argus hurried through his jobs, then obtained permission to go off on his own. With his heart beating he set out for the long line of sandhills in the distance, jogging and walking, his face pointing up as he sniffed the surf like an overjoyed dog.

When he reached the line of sandhills, about an hour from the camp, he found there were more dunes concealed behind them. His enthusiasm slowed a little as he climbed them, and then more hills. Sinking in and out of the sand at each step was tiring; it reminded him of times at home when he and his sister had played on the mud floors of dams that were drying up. When he did reach the final crest it came as a surprise: he had ceased to think about his reasons for ploughing through the endless sand.

But suddenly there it was — the wonderful ocean, fretting at the edge of a wonderful beach. Argus felt mad delight. He did not know what to look at first: the infinity of beach curving away to his left and right, or the infinity of flecked blue stretching out in front. He had never known before how something so empty could contain so much. He laughed and laughed. Making wild chortling noises, shedding his clothes and inhibitions, he ran down towards the edge of the water some distance away.

When he had thrown off his last piece of clothing he turned and ran backwards, pissing as he ran, wetting the sand in a pattern of huge zig-zags. A series of untidy somersaults then brought him to the ocean itself, and he stood with his feet in the water, watching the exhausted waves froth around his ankles. 'Fantastic!' he laughed excitedly. 'Fantastic! Fantastic!'

There was plenty of heat left in what had been a hot day, and Argus advanced a little further into the water, pushing against it with his shins. He looked around anxiously to make sure that he still had the beach to himself. Reassured, he waded on, gasping as waves broke against him, until he was up to his waist. 'Amazing,' he muttered to himself. He was now at the crucial point in the surf. Ahead of him the waves were breaking in agitated crashes; beyond was the calmness of the big swell. Behind him the breakers that had spent themselves in orgiastic climaxes were regrouping and surging again, in weak imitation of their earlier thunder; but Argus stood in the calm between the two lines of surf, exulting in the power of the water that broiled around his body.

Then, with a triumphant whoop he flung himself forward, lifting his knees and trying to run, charging at the roaring madness of white ahead of him. He reached it and flung himself into it; but he knew instantly, before his feet had even left the sand, that he had made a mistake, that here was a power beyond his experience and beyond his imagining. Suddenly, for the first time that he could remember, he had no control at all over what happened to him, no control over his body. The wave tossed him and rolled him and threw him around as though he were a rabbit held in the jaws of a dog, shaken furiously in all directions.

Even in the middle of the worst of it all, he knew that it would only last a few seconds, but those few seconds seemed never to end. And he failed to realise how quickly the next wave would be on him. As the maëlstrom passed he found the ocean floor with his feet again and stood up, gasping for breath and wiping the water from his eyes. No sooner had he done so than the next breaker exploded over him before he could see it. His lungs were still empty of air, and he found himself caught in another cauldron of white violence.

Argus was close to panic. He was thrown heavily into the sand. With no breath left in him he felt that he would not survive; if his first dumping had seemed to last a long time this second one was interminable. He was desperately tempted to open his mouth but still had enough reason left to resist. He knew he was in danger but did not know how to begin getting out of it. A vague instinct told him that someone would come and rescue him, but he also knew that the deserted beach could not suddenly grow people.

When the second wave had finished with him he had the sense to gulp some air before the onslaught of the third. To his relief it seemed less turbulent than the other two; he did not realise for a few moments that it was because an undertow was carrying him out to sea, but he understood what was happening when he tried to stand again in the wave's aftermath. He had a moment's sensation of slipping and thought he was going right under, but the water came to his neck, lapping under his chin as he desperately tried to keep his head up. Distracted by this, he did not think to gasp a proper breath again, and started to panic as he felt himself swept off his feet. This time it was not the cascading surf that was his enemy but the savage back-pull of the rip. Argus was helpless as it carried him, kicking and struggling, well out beyond the line of the breakers, so that he was floating in the big undulations of the swell. His head was an insignificant dot in the vast green movement of water.

Argus could swim; he and Sunday had swum many times in the dams and creeks of the farm, but this situation was very different. One of the dams at home — their favourite one — had been too deep in the middle for them to stand, but a few lazy strokes had always been sufficient to carry them to the shallows. And the water had always been passive — the swimmer was in control. Argus knew that he could float and tread water for a time, but he did not know if he could defeat the undertow, and he did not know how he would get through the surf again, assuming he could get that far.

As one of the swells lifted him Argus twisted around to get a glimpse of the beach. He was horrified to see how far away it was. He was also amazed to realise that he was being carried along to his left, and was now quite close to the headland. For the first time he became aware of cold, and could feel his limbs begin to tremble, not only with cold but also with fear. The boy strove to think clearly. What was he to do? Again his mind came close to being overwhelmed by panic. He had a momentary vision of his parents' faces when they heard the news that their other child was gone, and he recalled his father's voice, as clearly as though the man were at his shoulder now. And he remembered his father's favourite saying, one that had irritated the boy on many occasions in the past. 'Don't bring me problems, bring me solutions,' his father would say when Argus tried to tell him of a sheep that had got out onto the road, or a tree that had fallen on a fence, or a heifer that had sunk into the mud of a drying dam.

Now Argus summoned up the last shreds of his fragmented mind. What was the solution here? He tried a few experimental strokes towards the shore but knew he was making no progress. Then he tried swimming at a less direct angle and found that he was able to make some headway. But his body was shivering so much it was hard for him to make his limbs move vigorously again. He started yelling at himself through chattering teeth, abusing himself in an effort to get a response, trying to tap the reserves of energy that he knew would be there. His arms and legs slowly began to function, and even as his chest and muscles cried out in protest he began to make some progress.

After about ten or fifteen minutes Argus was drawing close to the wall of breaking waves again, but new problems were looming on his left, as he drifted steadily closer to the rocks at the end of the beach. By now he was swimming in a kind of fog of pain and weariness, in which his mind continued to function but was unable to motivate or inspire him. He was aware of the need to get through the breakers before he was carried onto the rocks, but it was his reflexes rather than his will that made his arms move faster and his legs kick harder.

In the event it proved to be easier than Argus had anticipated. The point at which he was attempting to come in had little undertow and, when he swam into the surf, his heart riddled with fear, the waves picked him up and carried him, so that he involuntarily became a bodysurfer, if a rather awkward one. He spoilt the ride quite quickly by attempting to stand up; he went sprawling on his knees, then rolled over in the froth and foam, but so great was his relief at feeling sand again that he did not mind its abrasive texture. He staggered to his feet and ran out of the water, still afraid of the way it pulled and strained at him, even though he knew that the danger was over.

Argus collapsed onto all fours on the damp sand, panting and sobbing like an animal. He knew how lucky he had been. Although he felt at first that he had not even the strength to stand, energy came back into his body more quickly than he expected, and after a few minutes he could walk back along the beach, to the spot where he had begun his swim in such carefree circumstances. The walk gradually warmed him and there was still plenty of daylight left when he reached his clothes. He dressed wearily thinking of the long hike still ahead of him. Suddenly he was feeling dizzy and weak. Yet he knew, as he had known in the water, that there was no rescue about to happen. No-one was about to drop out of the clouds and fly him back to the camp, or better still, back home. His fate was in his own hands; he had to get himself back to the security and warmth of Mayon's caravan. With a new maturity of determination he started on the first sandhill.

Chapter Ten

No-one ever heard how Argus had almost drowned on his first trip to the ocean. The people of the fair went about their own business each day without much interest in each other's doings. When Argus arrived back at the camp just after nightfall Temora commented that he looked tired and Mayon asked him if the coast had lived up to his expectations, but he just gave polite answers to both of them and pushed his way in to the communal soup pot that was simmering on the fire. After he had eaten he went straight to bed and slept for twelve hours without stirring.

In the morning Temora told him that she had come looking for him, to see if he wanted to take an early swim with her, but she had found him asleep. He was disappointed. Thinking back on the mistakes he had made in the surf, he was sure that he would be more successful the next time. Despite the danger, he was still exhilarated by his memories of the waves exploding around him. And the prospect of swimming with the beautiful Temora was exciting. He started to imagine the two of them running naked along the beach. He felt the blood start to race in his veins and his knees weaken beneath him and had to push the picture firmly out of his mind to get on with his decamping chores.

The convoy travelled parallel to the coast for about five more hours before arriving at Finauer, a fishing town situated on an inlet near the sea. It was a pretty place, smaller than Ifeka but still full of exotic new experiences for Argus. He had to work most of the night, however, getting the fair set up, and saw little of the town until the next day.

Soon enough, though, he and Temora went walking through the streets and down to the wharves. Most of the boats were out but there was still plenty of activity: old people mending nets, three boats up on slips being repaired and cleaned, children playing among the piles that supported the jetties. The two young people sat on the edge of one of the jetties and dangled their feet as they gazed down at the water.

'What do you think of the fair so far?' Argus asked.

'It's good. Some days you've got nothing to do, and other days you've got to work your butt off. Like last night. But I like it. What do you think of it?'

'I like it too,' Argus said. 'The first few days they were pretty unfriendly, except for Mayon and Jud. But they've been good since then. I think they just want to see if you're going to stay or not before they bother getting to know you. That's what Mayon said, anyway.'

'How long are you going to stay?' Temora asked.

'I don't know' the boy answered. 'A bit longer yet I guess. It's good because you get to see a few different places, and you get paid for doing it.'

'I know I'm not meant to ask,' Temora said hesitantly, 'but are you on your... you know...?'

'Yes,' Argus said quickly.

'I knew it!' the girl exulted. 'So am I.'

'Are you?' Argus asked, amazed. 'I thought you were too old. How old are you?'

'Fourteen,' Temora answered.

'Are you?' said Argus, 'I thought you were older than that . . . Where are you from?'

'Batlin.'

Argus knew that to be a city many times larger than Ifeka, away on the west coast. 'You've come a long way,' he said. 'What's it like?'

'Big,' the girl answered. 'It's where the River Ludi meets the Serembetter. We live right on the river, at a really nice spot where you can swim and fish.'

'Are there other children in your family?' Argus asked. 'I mean, if we're allowed to talk about things like that. I think we are.'

'We're allowed to talk about anything except the actual journey,' Temora said. 'That's so we don't use other people's experiences for our stories.'

'Were you told a lot about it, then?' Argus asked curiously.

'Oh yes,' the girl answered in surprise. 'Weren't you?'

'No, almost nothing. My parents didn't want me to go, but I picked up bits of information over the years from listening to the old men. And my father talked about his trip a bit when we were working out in the paddocks. But I didn't really get much, you know, formal instruction.'

'Didn't you?' Temora said. 'That's different from me. My father wasn't too keen but my mother was determined that I should go. She said it had been the best thing she'd ever done and she wanted me to do it too. But not many of my friends are going. They say it's too dangerous nowadays, especially for girls. But some of my friends are doing a sort of modified thing, where they go out and camp for a few days, things like that. But it's all pretty closely supervised. I don't think it'd be nearly as good.'

'So tell me about your family,' Argus said.

'Well ... I'm the oldest of five. I've got four little sisters. My father's an artist and my mother's a gardener. Um, what else can I tell you? My room is in a sort of attic, looking out over the river and there's an apple tree outside my window that I can reach when I'm hungry and can't be bothered going downstairs. My best friend's a girl called Pascall, who lives about a mile away. I've got a horse called Red and a dog called Cactus. They're both pretty slow, but then so am I sometimes ... I like cooking, and reading ... and riding Red. I like swimming and I like being on my own. I've got a tree that sticks out over the river and I go and sit in it when I want to do some thinking. Anyway ... that's enough about me. How about you?'

Argus was shy, cast into the unaccustomed role of talking about himself.

'Oh well,' he stammered. 'There's only one of me. I mean, I don't have any sisters or brothers.' But he felt a deep wrenching pain as he said that, and although he tried to control it, his face became contorted for a moment. 'We've got a farm up near Random. So we've got a few horses, and dogs too, though I've got my own special dog, called Dusty. I sort of help my parents on the farm. And I like most of the things you do ... reading, and being on my own, although there isn't much time for that because there's always so much work. It must be pretty hard for my father with me being away, but there's a fellow called Ranald who works for us when we're short.'

Without any spoken agreement the two got up and began walking along the shoreline. 'Do you get on with your parents?' Argus enquired.

'Yes,' Temora said a little hesitantly. 'I get on really well with my father, but my mother's a bit difficult. She always likes to get the last word. She's terrible to argue with. How about you?'

'I don't know,' Argus said honestly. 'My mother's quiet but we understand each other pretty well I think. My father — well, I guess I love him, but sometimes it's more like I hate him.' He thought about it a little further. 'I suppose I can tell I love him because of two things. One is that any time anyone criticises him — like, other people my age — I get really mad at them. And the other thing is that I know I'm proud of him, and all that he's achieved and I suppose being proud of someone must mean you love them, mustn't it?'

'Yes, I think so,' Temora agreed.

They stopped to watch a mother and two small children walking along the opposite bank of the inlet. One of the children broke away from his mother and ran towards the water, without the mother seeing.

'He's going to run straight into the water,' Temora said. But the child stopped at the edge and stood there peering at something. The mother, noticing at last that the child was missing, called to her truant son. But the boy, fascinated by whatever it was he was studying, would not acknowledge her until she had called out several times and was growing angry. And when he did answer, it was to say, 'Come and look Mummy, come and look.' The mother stayed where she was and kept calling; the child kept ignoring her, until the mother marched down to the water, bringing her other child with her, and dragged the little boy away by the arm.

'Good,' grunted Argus. 'He got what he deserved.'

But Temora laughed at him. 'You are a stick-in-the-mud,' she said. 'I'll tell you what that mother should have done. She should have gone down to the water, joined him in having a look at whatever he was so interested in, and then explained that it was time to continue with the walk. They had a confrontation that should never have happened. Two upset people — three, if you count the other child — and all so unnecessary. Like most confrontations.'

'Well, there's some you can't avoid,' Argus challenged. 'What about the other day, the last day at Ifeka, when that man in the tent started yelling stupid comments at Parara and Lavolta, and Jud told him to stop. That man was so unreasonable, no-one could have avoided that confrontation.'

'Well, I guess it's cheating to use hindsight,' Temora said. 'But I would have moved him out of the tent before I did anything. You know, get him somewhere else. Jud put him in a position where he was going to look weak in front of his friends. As soon as he did that, there had to be trouble.'

They walked on a little further.

'I'll tell you one thing,' said Argus presently. 'You know what I was saying before about love and hate, and how it's a bit of a mixture with my father.'

He picked up a stick and drew a long line on the ground, then drew a heart on one side and a dagger on the other.

'This is what it's like,' he said, and added in mock-didactic fashion: 'Are you concentrating now?' He went to one end of the line he had drawn and began walking along it, but strayed first on one side of it, then on the other.

'I get it,' Temora smiled.

'Well, it's exactly like that,' Argus said. 'I go from one to the other so quickly, and the line between them is so thin.'

'Yes,' said Temora. 'A very wealthy man from Batlin came to see my father one day. He spent half an hour telling my father how much he liked his work, what an admirer of my father he was, how he sang his praises all around the city. Then he offered my father a huge sum of money to paint his portrait, but my father refused, because he only paints faces that interest him. The man told my father he was a disagreeable untalented failure, and walked out. All it took was one word for him to cross that line that you've drawn, and that word was "No". In fact, when you think about it, "No" is probably the word that's most likely to send people from love to hate.'

'But "Yes" doesn't necessarily send them the other way,' Argus added. 'It must be hard being a parent, because you're always saying "No" to your kids, and sometimes they hate you for it. But you might be saying "No" for their own good, like if they want to go swimming in a spot that's dangerous,' he concluded, blushing a little as he nominated that as an example.

'Trouble is, they say "No" automatically,' Temora complained, 'without even thinking about it. That's what annoys me. Come on, we better get back. The fair opens at six and I want some tea first.'

Chapter Eleven

The next couple of days were busy, with some major jobs, including the re-roofing of a caravan and the construction of a new booth for the twins; their old one had been damaged in the altercation back at Ifeka. Argus added an extra touch to the booth: a lever system that would cause a flag to unfurl over the twins if they were in trouble and wanted to summon help. 'Thanks Argus, you're a sweet boy,' Parara said, but Lavolta merely commented, 'It's too complicated'.

Argus hardly noticed the crowds of people who filled the fairground these days — the crowds that had once contained him as an anonymous element. But he occasionally took the time to look at different faces, or to note the various vignettes that were being enacted at every moment: the child wheedling favours from a grandparent; the boy talking too loudly, to impress his friends; the tiny children who had not yet learnt to dissemble and whose faces showed every emotion; the farmer whose hands and face shone with the special scrubbing that only a trip 'to town' could induce; the warm hugs between people who knew each other well but who could meet only infrequently. Argus knew that these were universal scenes, recognisable anywhere, irrespective of time or place. He came to understand a little better what the book had meant when it spoke of stories that would be simultaneously one person's and all people's. There were moments when the boy, looking into the faces in the crowds as they passed him, could see beauty in each one — beauty so sharp and perfect it took his breath away. At such moments he knew he was in love with every person in the crowd, every person in the world, all humanity.

There was one person he was particularly attracted to, however, and that was Temora. He admired her intelligence and lively sense of humour, the friendliness she showed to everyone. And he felt inspired by the smooth lines of her body, and her clear fresh face. He tried writing poems about her when he was in bed at night, but gave up when his first efforts came out as either maudlin or clumsy. He started to find opportunities for them to be together, and indeed, his whole day began to be planned around her. For her part, she frequently sought him out or waited for him or came and sat next to him. The result was that they were together a good deal, even though they got teased for it.

On their last full day in Finauer they both had a free morning, and Temora seized the chance to extend the invitation she had nearly extended once before. She came into Mayon's caravan at about seven in the morning and woke Argus by pulling him out of bed by the feet.

'Go away!' cried Mayon crossly from his bed.

'What do you want?' asked Argus just as crossly, struggling to keep himself covered with the sheet he had nearly lost in the mêlée.

'Come to the coast with me,' said Temora, unperturbed by the chaos she had caused. 'We've got ages. We could do it easily. It's perfect weather for a swim.'

Argus was keen enough; he had not forgotten his earlier daydream of Temora naked on a beach. He grabbed some food and joined her outside the caravan. The day was already warming up and Argus quickly caught Temora's mood of excitement.

The distance was not much greater than it had been on Argus' previous trip to the surf. This time they simply followed the inlet, watching a late fishing boat ahead of them. When they reached the sea they turned to the south. They rounded a rocky headland and discovered beyond it a beach as perfect and unspoiled as the one Argus had been on less than a week earlier. They ran, giggling and excited, to the middle of it and flung themselves into the sand, rolling in it like otters in water.

'Have you got a swimming costume?' Temora asked.

'No,' Argus admitted.

'Good,' Temora announced, 'because neither have I.'

She jumped up and, turning away from the boy just a little, stripped off her few pieces of clothing and ran laughing towards the water. Argus, his heart pounding from the glimpses of her body, realised that if he did not hurry he would be left looking foolish. He threw off his shirt and pants and ran after her. He looked down at himself as he ran and was relieved to see that not only had his penis grown in recent weeks to a mature size, but also that it was behaving respectably given the circumstances it was now in. He splashed through the water after Temora, embarrassed enough to send up a big cloud of spray that would screen him for a few moments. But Temora seemed to be thinking only of swimming: she dived under one wave and over the top of the next, like a sleek porpoise at play.

Argus had swum and bathed many times with his sister and mother. But he had not realised the sheer beauty of a girl as perfectly proportioned as this one. As they swam around each other he stole what glances he could, fascinated by her unselfconscious nakedness. The surf was quite different from the earlier occasion that had nearly cost him his life. Now the waves were small and gentle. There was no undertow, and on this beach he was able to go a long way before getting out of his depth. He threw himself in and out of the breakers with no thought of anything but pleasure, revelling in the tingle and zest of the surf.

It was nearly an hour before he decided he was cold and tired enough to stop. He jogged out of the water to where their discarded clothes lay like giant butterfly wings on the sand. He stretched out on his back and watched Temora. After a few minutes more she too left the water and walked up to him, without haste or concealment, and lay down, laughing and dripping.

'Oh, it's fantastic,' she said. 'I wish we could do this every day.'

Argus became aware that his body was no longer behaving respectably. He rolled over onto his front, Temora was too quick for him. She leant over and pushed him, continuing the roll, so that he ended on his back again. She was giggling as she inspected him and reached out with a tentative finger to touch him. Argus lay still, afraid that if he moved, or breathed, she might stop. But she continued to tease with her light fingers. 'Oh,' Argus sighed. To himself he thought, 'Oh, this is too much.' While he had the strength still in him he turned sideways to her and ran his hands along her body. She was smooth, like music, smooth like mahogany.

The sand, the sky, the ocean, all became lost, all were absorbed within the two of them on the beach. Argus could not believe what he was feeling. Even the touch of a breeze was a caress, a tantalizing feather drawn down his bare skin. Everything was a source of wonder to him — the wetness, the curling hair, the opening, the slow opening before him, the slow cry of the seagull from the wet sand.

Argus felt as though his fingers had gained a new sensitivity. He could feel the blood stirring in her body, the growing heat, the yearning that suffused her being. As they moved together the weight of his excitement went before him. All that he was feeling was centred in it and had taken him over; it did the exploring for him. He ceased to think; he only floated.

Afterwards the two of them stayed together, Argus enjoying the most complete relaxation he had ever known, as Temora's hand stroked up and down his back. It was a sweet contentment. He drifted into a kind of sleep for a few minutes, aware of every movement around him but unable to stir.

At last they separated and lay side by side on the beach. 'Oh it's amazing,' Argus said.

Temora giggled. 'They sent us on this journey so we could become women,' she mused. 'Or men, as the case may be. Do you think this is what they meant?'

Argus sat up and gazed frankly at her as she brushed the sand from her sides and back. The sight was enough to induce new excitement in him.

'Oh no you don't,' said Temora, glancing across. But she watched with pleasure as he again reached his zenith. 'Do you want some more?' she asked curiously. When he nodded she knelt up and began stroking him with gentle hands.

'This'll do it, won't it?' she asked. 'I remember when we were little kids, playing with our cousins. We used to do this to them and they'd go through the roof.'

Argus went through the sky and the heavens at her touch, until all too soon he was gasping with the familiar sweet pain. 'No more, no more,' he said, pushing her hand away. Temora sat back on her heels.

'Well,' she said, 'girls and boys sure are different. Did that feel good?'

'Yes thanks,' Argus said, as though he had been handed a mug of tea.

By common accord, without either needing to say anything, they both suddenly leapt up and ran for the water again, throwing themselves into the surf with wild splashes. But this time five minutes was enough, before they returned to their clothes to dry themselves.

'It's time to go,' said Argus, pulling on his trousers. 'We'll have to step it out.' He waited for Temora and shyly took her hand as they set off around the headland on their walk back to the fair site.

Chapter Twelve

'Here, I'll help you,' Argus said, late one night, watching Tiresias trying to carry two saucepans, a chair and a blanket back from the fire to his caravan. He took the chair and followed the dark, silent figure to his home, which was parked, as always, a little away from the tents and other caravans. When they reached the van Tiresias opened the door and put his things inside. He turned and took the chair from Argus, then went back and closed the door in the boy's face, all without a word. Argus had been trying to get a surreptitious glance inside but was only able to gain a blurred impression of red curtains and an over-clean neatness. He went back to the fire feeling rather disgruntled.

'He didn't even thank me,' he complained to Mayon.

'Why should he?' Mayon asked. He was in a provocative mood.

'Well, he just should. Good manners,' Argus said. 'I did him a favour, and he's supposed to thank me.'

'Listen, boyo,' said Mayon. 'What's all this "should" and "supposed to" stuff? We're talking about people here, human beings. "Should" and "meant to" don't apply. Once you start to formulate codes of behaviour and decide that everyone has to abide by them, and that those who don't are rude or ignorant or bad, then you've lost sight of what people are. Tell me, why did you help Tiresias by offering to carry his chair?'

'I felt sorry for him,' Argus said promptly. 'He was getting in such a mess, and I thought it'd be nice to give him a hand.'

'All right, now tell me another reason.'

'I felt bad that we don't get on very well and I thought it might help him understand that I don't dislike him,' Argus said, not quite as promptly.

'Do you dislike him?'

'Well, not dislike him exactly, but I don't like him all that much. He's so unfriendly. I feel sorry for him, but he makes me a bit nervous.'

'Now tell me another reason for carrying the chair.'

'Um ... I wanted to see what the inside of his caravan looked like, 'cos he's always so secretive.'

'Right. Next one.'

Blushing, but laughing a little at himself, Argus hung his head and said, 'I wanted everyone around the fire to see what a good fellow and helpful person I am. Especially because I've been pretty lazy today, and I thought people might be a bit angry at me.'

Mayon laughed with him. 'You're certainly honest,' he said. 'Now, what does all that tell you?'

'That everything's much more complicated than it first seems,' Argus said, remembering the old leather-covered book back at the farmhouse, a long long time ago. 'Nothing's simple.'

'Yes, that line sounds familiar,' Mayon commented. 'And that's a good start. But what else can you say?'

Argus considered for a few moments, then decided what

he wanted to say. 'What I don't like about all this,' he said, 'is that it makes me wonder if there's any such thing as people being kind to each other, just for the sake of being kind. You know, "being good", which we're always told to be. Does "good" mean anything at all?'

Mayon shrugged. 'It'd be very convenient if everything was as simple as that. The world would be a simple place. But shallow and two-dimensional as well. I mean, when two people look at a pond, who has the richer view? The one who sees the pretty sheet of water, or the one who also sees the rich life teeming in the depths and around the edges? Is it better to be ignorant and happy, or wise and sad? Assuming those words go together, which of course they often don't. I don't know what the answer is to the question, and indeed the question is too "black and white" to be worth much, but I do know that as soon as you start to formulate rules and laws and codes of behaviour you're in trouble. And that goes for something as simple as a system of manners. Because they don't allow for the complexity of each situation, nor for the fact that each situation is so different. Your carrying of the chair, for example. If you'd carried it a day earlier or a day later, or if you'd carried it for someone else, or if someone else carried the chair for Tiresias — then a whole different set of factors would have come into play.' Mayon paused for breath.

'But you have to have rules and laws,' Argus objected. 'I mean, there are some situations that are just bad, and so one law can cover them.'

'Such as?' Mayon asked.

'Well, killing,' Argus said. 'I mean, killing someone's always wrong.' He paused a moment and thought, trying to see his statement through the glasses that Mayon was providing. 'No, I guess not,' he concluded reluctantly.

'Why not then?' Mayon prompted.

'Well,' Argus said, 'because every case is different. Sometimes the person gets provoked into doing it. Or the person who does it might be a bit mad in the head, so they don't know what they're doing. Or someone might have been brought up to be violent, or without any self-discipline; so even though the killing is wrong, the killer can't be blamed much.'

'Yes, good,' Mayon agreed. 'Also, there are so many different situations in which one person might end the life of another. There's the soldier on the battlefield, for example. He is probably in a different category from a person who murders for money. And then there's the man I knew once, who owned a fishing boat and worked from a port near here. He would fish a long way out, three or four days' journey from his home. When his little son was old enough he would accompany his father and help as much as he could. But, one night the candle they were using started a fire. The little boy's clothing caught alight, and he was frightfully burnt. The father knew a little medicine and realised that the boy could not survive the three day trip back to port. He knew the boy would die in appalling agony, and so he took a pillow and ended his son's life.'

'And if someone's about to hurt you or kill you, or hurt someone in your family,' Argus said, 'you might kill them then, if there was no other way out of it.'

'We've come a long way from you carrying a chair for Tiresias,' Mayon laughed.

'I still think he's a weird person,' Argus commented.

Mayon was exasperated. 'Then you've learnt nothing from this conversation! When you say "weird", you mean he doesn't match up to your set of "rules" for human beings — rules that are impossible, inappropriate, and which ignore everything you've come to understand about people!' He cuffed the boy lightly but affectionately on the head. 'Go and check the performance area. I'm going to bed.'

Argus ambled away into the dark, his mind in a turmoil. He wondered if one day he would figure it all out, understand everything, but a quick glance up at the stars reminded him most emphatically that he wouldn't. He tightened a few ropes on the main tent and picked up some rubbish that was blowing around, then he too went to bed. He dreamt that night that he was walking through a huge house of many storeys. The higher he went in the house, the steeper and more difficult the stairs became, and the more cluttered were the rooms. But each succeeding room was also full of richer and more fascinating treasures. When he woke in the morning and recalled the dream, Argus needed no help in understanding what it meant.

Chapter Thirteen

Argus and Temora walked miles and miles along the sand. At times they had to scramble across rocks to get around the headlands, but usually they were able to enjoy the fine white powder that lay warm under their feet. Three weeks had passed since their passionate afternoon near Finauer; the fair was about to turn inland again, on a route that would take it a long way from the coast. On their only afternoon off in the area, the two young people had decided to enjoy a last sight of the sea.

In three weeks they had formed a close friendship that they both valued. The fair had been moving quite quickly through a number of small fishing towns, so the work had been hard and the hours long. The turnover of stringers had been so heavy that Argus was now Jud's longest-serving employee. Often they had been short-staffed and everyone had to take on extra duties. Argus had grown to respect Temora's cheerful serenity, her ready grasp of detail, her willingness to work without complaint for lengthy stretches of time. When he was tired his spirits were often raised by her cobbled laughter.

At first they had been teased often about their friendship, especially by Ruth, and by the twins, Lavolta and Parara.

Condemned to a life in which normal relationships were impossible, the twins, Parara in particular, were fascinated by other people's affairs. After a few days, however, the teasing stopped, as new matters came along to claim the general interest. In fact Argus and Temora had not had many opportunities to be alone together. When they were alone, the conversation was sometimes faltering and stilted, sometimes flowing and easy. The same was true of their physical relationship. There were days when neither of them wanted to touch each other. There were days when one was in an erotic mood but the other wasn't. On a couple of memorable occasions both had delighted in the pleasure they could give each other. Sometimes when they had been talking late into the night in Temora's tent Argus would end up sleeping there but, despite Jud's sly innuendos, on most of these occasions they just enjoyed the comfort of having a warm body to hug and hold.

Now, on the beach, they were roaming far and wide, racing across long expanses of sand to throw shells at seagulls or to examine unusual clumps of seaweed. And then they would walk side by side, talking about anything and everything. 'You know,' said Argus on one of these occasions, 'the whitest things in the world are seagulls, milk and fresh snow. They're the three whitest things.'

On one headland the rocks were piled up in huge jumbles and the waves beat furiously against them. The air was full of spray and an invisible vapour danced on the faces of Argus and Temora, as they watched from a distance. 'All that power and noise,' Temora said. 'It looks like the water's not doing anything, but it always wins in the end. It might take centuries, but it wears those rocks away, sooner or later.'

'Imagine if you could harness the power,' Argus said. 'That'd be something. You could do a lot with that.'

It was difficult to get around the headland, and they were nearly inclined to give up and go back, feeling they had come far enough already. But Argus' suggestion that they should do just that was turned down by Temora. 'No, come on' she said, laughing, 'there could be something magical on the other side.' So they inched their way up a crack in a rock, and crawled over a long, dangerously smooth and slippery section, then squeezed through some narrow gaps, until Temora, who was leading, gave a triumphant shout and cascaded down a sandhill onto the new beach.

This was a beach different from any other they had come across. It was quite small, and very beautiful: a stream of fresh water coming down a fern-lined gully had enabled the dark-green vegetation to grow right to the edge of the sand. It was rockier than the other beaches too, and its surrounds were riddled with dark holes that indicated caves. The outstanding feature though, compared to any other part of the coastline they had been on, was the evidence of a human presence. In the fringe of palms and grass and bushes along the treeline was a hut built of roughly hewn timber and driftwood, with two glassless windows that gazed at the unknowing ocean. A hessian curtain flapped idly in the sea breeze, unchecked by any human hand. A homemade chair sat empty by the front door, also facing the waves. Seagulls stalked the beach, pecking angrily at the heavy wet sand. Nothing else moved.

'Let's go,' said Temora. 'I don't like the look of this.' But there was nothing in her voice to suggest that she really wanted to go, and she made no movement back towards the headland. When Argus began walking towards the hut, she followed readily enough.

They came to the door of the hut and stood about two body-lengths from it, trying to see in to the black interior. 'Is anyone there?' Argus called out nervously. There was no answer. He took a few more steps forward and peered through the doorway. 'I think there is someone there, asleep,' he said to Temora, who was looking over his shoulder. He knocked loudly on the wooden frame, hurting his knuckles a little in doing so. As his eyes became accustomed to the darkness he could see there was indeed someone stretched out on a camp bed against a side wall. Argus knocked again, and called, 'Hello! Anyone home?'

'Maybe he's dead,' Temora said, and giggled.

'Don't laugh,' Argus said grimly. 'I think he might be.'

Temora gasped, and Argus stepped gingerly into the hut and over to the bed. One look at the open mouth and staring eyes of the figure on the bed told him all that he needed to know. Temora, now framed darkly in the doorway, asked, 'Is he?'

'Yes,' said Argus, 'only it's not a he, it's a she.'

'Oh, no,' said Temora, 'I've never seen a dead body.'

'Well, now's your chance,' said Argus, aware that he was hardly acting appropriately, but not sure what he should be feeling. Temora came forward and stood beside him, gazing in fascination, her hand over her mouth.

'What do you think she died of?' Temora asked.

'I don't know,' Argus answered, 'but she looks pretty old.'

He picked up the cold white hand that hung lifeless beside the bed and placed it across the woman's chest, linking it with the other hand that was already there. Then, not without some revulsion, he closed the tired eyes and tried to close the slack mouth, but without success. Temora took a cloth from a washstand and soaked it in a nearby bucket of water, then gently wiped the dried white saliva from around the mouth. They looked helplessly at each other.

'What do we do now?' Argus asked.

'I don't know. Take the blanket off and see if she had any bad injuries or anything.'

Argus lifted the hands while Temora peeled off the blanket. Argus was praying that she would not be naked but she was dressed in a rough shift made of brightly coloured material. Though there were no signs of obvious trauma her legs were covered with many old scars and burns, that showed up pale against the dark tanned skin. Her feet were bare.

'Well, I don't know what she died of,' Temora said.

'Guess it doesn't matter,' Argus answered. 'It doesn't matter to her now, anyway.' He folded the blanket and put it on an old box that sat next to the bed and they stood looking down at the body.

'It's amazing,' said Temora. 'She seems so... sort of colourless. Not white, just colourless, the way water has no colour. I'm not scared of her any more but I can't say she's exactly an attractive sight. Her skin feels a bit clammy.'

'She looks like she'd have been a nice old lady though,' said Argus. 'I mean, it's a bit hard to say with her mouth the way it is, but she looks sort of kind. Not that you can ever tell, of course.'

Temora was starting to take an interest in the contents of the little hut. Apart from the bed and box and washstand the single room dwelling contained only an improvised table, made out of planks, a couple of stools, and a number of other trunks and boxes that served as cupboards. The decorations were simple: a painting of a boat, done in a child's hand, but old and faded; a broken doll, one-eyed and battered; a couple of bottles containing flowers; some shells and pebbles; and a dried flower arrangement. The only features that were really striking were a number of beautifully-worked pieces of embroidery hung around the walls and piled on top of one of the boxes. The scenes they depicted were of children: children dressed in vivid clothes; children at work; children on a beach; children playing musical instruments and dancing.

Temora and Argus looked through the pile of pieces on the box, lost in admiration. Both were aware that they had never seen more skilful work. The designs and the execution were the work of a great artist. 'Maybe she had children and lost them?' Argus ventured.

'Mmmm,' Temora said. 'These are amazing. My mother does embroidery but she'd give up if she ever saw these. Look at that doll.' She pointed to a broken doll that had been worked into one of the pieces, a perfect miniature of the doll perched on the window-sill of the hut.

Argus started to open some of the boxes and chests. The first one contained only a jumble of clothes; the second a collection of books that seemed to be mainly poetry and which showed evidence of having been well-read. Other boxes held cooking and eating utensils and food. But it was the last box, nearest the bed, that revealed something of a personal nature. There were various curios, oddments, bits of jewellery, and a packet of papers.

'I don't know if we ought to be doing this,' said Temora

uneasily, as Argus pulled out the papers and began to open them.

Argus shrugged. 'Looks like she's all alone. I don't imagine she'd have visitors from one year to the next. We should at least try to find out who she is.' He unrolled a sheet of paper and, after glancing over it, began reading out loud:

> My boat moves out through the harbour.
> I slip like a ghost past the bar.
> I catch the wind at the headland
> And steer by the evening star.
>
> My vessel is stormed at by water
> That tears at my sheets and my sails.
> My bow is lost in the furrows
> As water floods over the rails.
>
> But it's storms that give me my reason
> And darkness that strengthens my sight.
> From days of sweet calm I learn patience.
> I sail unafraid into night.
>
> I'm not a hunter or trader.
> I go where I must, at the call.
> The treasure of death still awaits me,
> A dark, golden world to explore.

They were both silent for a few moments. 'It's hard to believe,' Temora said at last, 'that she could have written anything like that, the way she's lying there now.' Argus continued to sort through the papers. There were more poems, and a packet of sketches, mainly of sea-birds, executed amateurishly but with a loving touch. About half the pile seemed to consist of letters. Argus started to read one but then stopped almost at once, and parcelled them up again. 'It doesn't seem right,' he said.

Temora had found a very old, very solid brass magnifying glass, and was using it to examine a ring set with a deep red stone. 'Beulah,' she announced, reading an inscription on the inside of the ring. 'That must be her name.'

'Yes, I saw it on one of the letters,' Argus agreed. Temora continued to pick through the collection of items admiring a carved wooden elephant, and lingering over a necklace of coral and rose quartz. But at last she had satisfied her curiosity and, putting the lid back on the box, she went in search of Argus, who was no longer in the hut.

She found him outside, digging a grave in the soil behind the little shack. 'Are there any more spades?' she asked.

'Don't think so,' he answered. 'Found this one behind the front door. But you could make something to put on the grave, if you want. Flowers and stuff.'

Temora, who was quick and skilful with a knife, found one and carved into a piece of wood the name 'Beulah' and the date, then collected a garland of white and yellow flowers.

By this time Argus had finished digging in the sandy soil, and so, with some trepidation, the two entered the hut again and tried to lift the body from the bed. It proved to be unexpectedly heavy and surprisingly floppy, so they laid it back down and slid the blanket underneath. This was more successful, but even so there was little dignity about the old woman's final journey, as they sweated and

strained to get her out through the door, bumping themselves and the body a number of times. At the graveside
they lowered her with more solemnity into the open pit
and then, embarrassed by her haggard face, they closed
the blanket over her.

'We should say something,' said Argus.

'Yes, but what?'

'I remember a sentence from when my sister was buried... I thought it was the most beautiful sentence I'd
ever heard. "Rest perpetual grant unto her, and may light
eternal shine upon her." And we could read her poem.'

'Yes, I'll get it,' Temora agreed, and slipped into the
hut.

Argus looked down at the shape in the blanket. 'Good-
bye Beulah, if that was your name,' he said. 'I think you
were probably a very nice person, but maybe not a happy
one. I wish I'd known you while you were alive, but I
guess I've got to know you a little bit now.'

Temora re-emerged with the poem, and read it with
clarity and feeling. She picked up the spade and, not
without some hesitation, cast a shovelful of soil into the
grave. She laboured on without speaking until the job
was finished, then Argus placed the carved inscription and
the flowers on the mound. 'We'd better go,' he said. 'We'll
be late enough as it is.'

'Wait a minute,' Temora said. 'I think we should leave
a message here, saying what we've done, in case anyone
does ever turn up to see her. I mean, she might have
an estranged son who she hasn't seen for twenty years,
since he ran away to sea, and he might get shipwrecked
on this very coast, and stagger into the hut expecting to
find her waiting for him.'

'Yes, she might,' Argus agreed, sounding far from convinced. 'Still, it's a good idea.'

Between them they managed to write a statement of what they had found in the hut and of the actions they had taken. They broke up all the perishable food and threw it onto the beach for the seagulls. Then Temora handed Argus a thick, very plain silver ring, as she slipped an identical one on her own finger.

'What's this?' he said, in surprise.

'Her rings,' Temora explained. 'They were next to the bucket of water, and she had marks on her fingers where she wore them. I think they were the only pieces of jewellery she wore, so they must have been the only ones she cared about. I think we should wear them from now on, so that we remember her and she's still got a little part of her left with us. 'Cos I don't think she had anyone else.'

'All right,' Argus said, 'but we better add a postscript to our note, saying that we've taken them.'

This task completed, they closed the door behind them, and set off for the headland, without a backward glance. The last half of their journey to the fairground was a struggle. They both ran out of energy at about the same time, and they stumbled into the light of Mayon's fire feeling hungry and depressed and very very tired.

Chapter Fourteen

A week later, camped at the great trading centre of Bratten, the members of the fair prepared to enjoy themselves. Bratten was at the junction of two major rivers and three great highways. Argus thought he had never seen so many people before in his life. They crowded into the fairground all day and half the night, and Argus and Temora were needed almost constantly. A typical morning might have one of them in charge of a throwing game, then acting as cashier for the freakshow, or cleaning up rubbish, before taking lunches around to people too busy to leave their posts. Sometimes too Argus would be called on to help Jud eject a trouble-maker, or patrol an area where the crowd was over-boisterous. As other stringers came and went, Argus found himself often in charge of people older than him. He had a few difficulties at first, until he learnt to identify the assertive ones. He made a point of being more assertive than they were, so that he got their respect, if not their liking.

For Bratten, this was the most important week of the year, as the district celebrated its Festival of the Gift. The fair was closed on the final day of the Festival, when the people went to the river for the Silence. But Argus and Temora and most of the people from the fair were too tired to go. They spent the day making a few desultory repairs, washing clothes, lazing about. Around dusk nearly everyone drifted in to the communal fire, and a massive stew started to take form. Ruth sliced potatoes and Argus, the only one who could do it without weeping, chopped onions. Tiresias came out of the shadows of his caravan to throw in handfuls of herbs of some kind.

'What are they?' Argus asked, but Tiresias only smiled and shrugged. Titius, the human skeleton, as usual contributed nothing but advice, most of it bad. Delta and Cassim, the two women storytellers, arrived from the paddocks with aprons full of fresh mushrooms, which were received with delight. Mayon added his special tomato blend: he claimed it was from a recipe he had dreamed while asleep in a cave full of carnivorous lizards. Temora's contribution was a huge quantity of garlic.

The atmosphere was good, light-hearted and casual. People who had been taking each other for granted realised with sudden pleasure how much real affection and warmth they shared, and were suddenly delighted to see someone with whom they had been fighting a few days earlier. Even Tiresias unbent and became quite playful. One of the inevitable dogs that hung around the fair trotted close to the fire and tried to sniff the stew. Tiresias made as if to lift it up and toss it in to the pot; the dog yelped, squirmed free and made off. Everyone laughed; the tremor of shared laughter ran through the group.

After they had fed and were warmed by the excellent meal, the members of the fair sat around the fire, not wanting to leave, in a mood for sharing confidences. Mayon, who had been brought up on a farm, was telling a story of his own childhood. Argus, who had been washing plates did not hear the start of it, but arrived in time for the climax. 'When we went to dig the cattle out of the mud,' he said, 'we didn't know that the ones we could see were only the top layer. As we got them out, we realised there were more underneath. I don't know how many layers there were. But the smell, oh the smell. I'll never forget it. It took days to get them all, even using a winch. That was a bad drought, that one.'

Cassim chimed in. 'Yes,' she said, 'there are some memories that depend on smells, I think. When I was about ten we had a fire at home. We were shearing at the time, and we were down to the last mob of sheep... about a hundred, I think. We put them in the shed for the night, so if it rained they'd still be dry in the morning. We went back to the house, had tea and went to bed early... you know how tiring shearing can be. And when we woke up in the morning, there was a funny smell. We went over to the shearing shed. It was quite a walk from the house, behind a row of trees. There was nothing there except a pile of smoking embers. It had burnt down during the night, with all the sheep inside, and being so far from the house nobody heard a thing. That's a smell I'll never forget.'

'Must have been a bit more than a pile of smoking embers,' Jud observed after a few moments silence, while people digested the story and tried to imagine themselves into it.

'Well, yes,' Cassim admitted. 'That was a bit exaggerated. But most good stories are. Some of the sheep — quite a lot actually — were relatively undamaged. They were buried under others in corners of the shed, where they'd huddled to escape the flames, and they'd died of suffocation, I suppose. We were able to shear them and sell the wool, but that was the only thing salvaged out of the ruins.'

'You could shear the dead sheep?' Ruth asked in amazement.

'Yes, of course. But it's an awkward job. Not as awkward as burying them though. We had to dig an enormous pit. For the rest of the time that we lived on that farm I didn't like to go near the site of the pit.'

'It's terrible when animals die,' Ruth agreed. 'They don't understand what's happening to them, whereas humans do. Maybe that's one of the differences between animals and humans. Humans know that one day they have to die, but I don't think animals know that.'

'I don't know which is worse,' Cassim said.

'Some animals understand,' Tiresias said quietly. Unnoticed by Argus he had drawn closer to the fire. The flames were reflecting on his dark face. 'Elephants understand.'

'Elephants?' Temora asked, a little astonished.

'Yes, elephants,' Tiresias repeated. 'I've seen an elephant deliberately sacrifice its own life to save another, and I believe that it knew what it was doing.'

'Tell us,' someone said, but Tiresias, unaccustomed to speaking in front of others, paused a long while before going on.

'Many years ago,' he finally began, 'I was watching a big herd of elephants grazing at the bottom of quite a steep cliff. Near me was a family group — a mother and three of her calves. The oldest was perhaps four or five. Suddenly I heard a rumble like distant thunder and at the same time the ground began to tremble. The elephants looked around them in fear, as indeed I did. But it was from above that the danger was coming. High above us a landslide had started, and was coming down a funnel in the rock with frightening speed. The shape of the funnel meant that the landslide itself was restricted to a narrow area, and I was well clear of its path. But the big cow elephant was not. She had been feeding a little bit away from her calves, and a massive boulder the size of a caravan was hurtling towards her. It was at the heart of the landslide, but the old elephant, confused by the echoes coming off the cliffs opposite us, did not see it. Her oldest calf saw it, however. Flinging his trunk in the air and lifting his front feet, he charged across the empty ground and threw himself in front of the boulder. He took the full impact of it. It killed him instantly, I think, but he slowed its progress and by then his mother had time to get out of the way.'

'What happened then?' Ruth asked. Argus suppressed a giggle at the thought that Ruth of all people would be concerned about elephants.

'Well, the other members of the herd reacted the way elephants nearly always react when they come across a dead or dying elephant. They gathered around him and tried to lift him with their tusks and trunks. The mother seemed to be especially distressed. They stayed around him for the rest of the day and, although some would wander off for a few hours, they would always come back. At times there would be a circle of elephants around the corpse, packed so tightly that I couldn't see what they were doing; at other times there'd only be one or two. Late in the afternoon one of the big bulls seemed to be tugging at the tusks of the dead calf, as though he wanted to remove them. I'd heard of that happening, but I'd never seen it before. Anyway, if that's what he was trying to do, he was unsuccessful, and round about dusk they ambled away, although some still lingered till well after dark. When I came back the next morning, they'd covered the body with branches and mud.'

'Oh, that can't be true,' Mayon protested.

Tiresias smiled. 'It's amusing to hear a storyteller objecting to a story on those grounds. Nevertheless it is true and it's quite common behaviour among elephants. And that's not the only thing about them that surprises people. For instance, with this calf I was telling you about, for six weeks or so, every elephant that passed that spot would come over and inspect the body, even if they were from a different herd. And, as the process of decomposition took over, the elephants would frequently pick up bones and wave them around as though they were examining them. Don't ask me what they were doing. I've never been able to explain it and I've never met anyone else who's able to either.'

'What were you doing around elephants?' Temora hazarded.

'I was brought up around them,' Tiresias answered simply. 'I lived in a village where every night baboons raided our garden and butterflies bigger than my hand filled the morning air. My baby brother was put out in his cot in the sun one day, for some fresh air, and his nurse left him for a few moments while she finished washing the clothes, and that was the last anyone saw of him. He had disappeared, and even the widest searches failed to reveal any traces. Then, when I was eight, I was taken too, but I was taken by men and I think he was taken by animals. I was smuggled across the seas, and have never seen my family or village since.'

There was a long pause, broken by Ruth, who gave a loud sniff and blew her nose into a handkerchief. 'Oh dear, that's so sad,' she said. 'I feel so lucky. I was such a happy little girl, and I do feel awful when I hear a story like that. We don't know when we're well off, and that's a fact.'

'How did you get into this way of life?' Delta asked her.

'Well, dear, my parents died when I was young, about fifteen. They caught an illness that went right through the valley where we lived. Lots of people caught it, and they all died. No-one knew what caused it, and I don't know even now, but one day they were well and happy, and the next day they were both dead. So I buried them and then went to stay with my uncle and his family who lived up in the mountains. But they were too stern and strict for me. I liked my bit of fun. And I was already pretty big. I just seemed to put weight on quickly — in a year or two I went from average plump to not much less than you see now. Well, as soon as I saw the fair I knew it was for me. It was the only way I could be looked after comfortably and enjoy the kind of life I wanted. And I must say I've never regretted it. It was Felder, the father of Jud and Mayon, who ran it in those days, and he was the one who hired me, and he always took very good care of me.'

'Haven't you ever wanted to do anything different?' Temora asked.

'Oh my dear!' Ruth chuckled. 'Yes of course I have my dreams. Don't we all? I'd love to be a dancer or a poet or a shepherd. But I'm in a very nice groove with the fair now, and I don't want to have to make a whole lot of changes.'

'The wanderer's danger is to find comfort,' Mayon quoted softly, so that only Argus and Temora could hear. Temora looked at him long and thoughtfully, then got to her feet and strolled off in the direction of her tent. The conversation around the fire switched to the favourite topic of the human oddities who peopled the fair: illness. They could discuss their health for hours, each willing to pay the price of listening to the others' medical histories on the understanding that the others in turn would listen to theirs. Argus, quickly tiring of the tedious subject, quit for the evening and went to bed.

Chapter Fifteen

Two days later Temora left the fair to begin her journey home. Though she did not mention it, Argus felt that Mayon's muttered aside at the fire had helped her to make her decision.

Although she was travelling in the general direction of her home, she was leaving the fair when it was furthest away from Batlin, and the route she planned appeared to be a particularly arduous one. But she was adamant that it was time for her to move on, and she would not discuss the decision with Argus. Indeed, she seemed preoccupied, as though she had already closed Argus out of her life, and the boy's depression as he moped around the campsite had so little apparent effect on her that Argus started to grow angry.

But when the time came for her to go she became once more, for a few minutes that Argus cherished long afterwards, her former self. She flung her arms around him, gave him a wicked kiss and laughed with a reckless pleasure. 'Oh, I'm so glad I met you,' she said. 'I'll never forget that day on the beach. And the times in the tent, and the caravan. If I ever have another boyfriend I'll always be comparing him to you, and he'll never know why I suddenly seem to be twenty years away.'

Argus laughed, despite himself. 'I'll miss you too,' he said, and meant it, though after her familiar figure had finally vanished around a corner in the road he felt a strange sense of what seemed almost like relief. He quickly suppressed the feeling, not liking to admit that although he liked Temora he was glad to be free of such a long and intense relationship.

Her departure nudged Argus into the realisation that he must also be moving on. 'The wanderer's danger is to find comfort.' He was, and must continue to be, a wanderer and, although the end of his quest was starting to take shape in the distance, he still had a way to go yet. He broached the subject with Mayon as they were setting up at their newest venue, the city of Palatine.

It was not easy for him to tell the storyteller his decision, for he had grown to look on the gentle Mayon as a second father, and he knew that Mayon cared for him as a son. Yet the storyteller only hesitated a moment before agreeing with the boy that there was nothing more the people of the fair could teach him. At first Argus promised to stay on until they left Palatine, but once he had made up his mind to go, he found himself becoming unbearably restless, and Mayon, sensing this, gave him permission to leave as soon as a replacement could be found. This did not take long in a city the size of Palatine, and so it came about that on a wet and grey-cold morning Argus slung his blanket-roll on his back and took to the roads once more.

His departure was an emotional affair for everyone, though the people of the fair, accustomed to comings and goings, probably recovered more quickly than Argus. He shook hands gravely with Tiresias, Titius and Jud, kissed the two twins on their cheeks, and was smothered in a bear hug by Ruth. Then he and Mayon walked a little way down the road together.

'It's been good,' Argus said, feeling suddenly shy. 'They're good people.'

'They're a mixture of good and bad, like everyone else,' Mayon answered with a smile. 'But there's one thing you still haven't figured out about them.'

'What's that?' Argus asked in surprise.

Mayon shrugged. 'They're all you, all a different part of you. Well, this is far enough for me. I hope our paths cross again. Goodbye Argus. Take care, as people say, but take risks too.' The two embraced, as both felt tears smart in their eyes.

'Goodbye,' Argus said. 'Thank you so much. Good-bye.'

And so it was now Argus' turn to walk away, as Temora had done so recently and Mayon's turn to stand and watch. But Argus' direction was the opposite of Temora's: his route led him inland, where hers had been towards the coast.

It took him some time to get back into the pace and rhythm he had developed before joining the fair. But he was glad to be on his own again, and realised he had been getting stale, physically and mentally.

For the first time in quite a while he began observing the countryside around him. He was still in cleared and arable land, of a type that had become familiar to him, but the further he went from Palatine the more the gradient increased, and the less inviting was the general prospect. After a few hours he was puffing a little, climbing into the hills and gaining height rapidly as the road twisted around. At length he paused at an escarpment and looked out at the plains he was leaving. The city of Palatine lay dark and heavy between him and the horizon. He could see the tents and caravans of the fair but he was able to look at them without too great a sense of loss.

Far in the distance was the ocean, almost flippant in its light blue insignificance. He laughed aloud as he thought of the memories and associations that the sea now held for him. It would be a part of his life forever. Other towns and villages were scattered across the countryside. Most of them were alien to Argus, and he wondered for a moment how it could be that they held individuals and families whom he would never meet or even see. Yet to them their lives were all-important, they were the suns in their local solar systems. How could they be oblivious of him, and for that matter, how could he be oblivious of them? A person's life, his or her living and dying, were too important to be carried out in anonymity.

Argus sighed and turned away, resuming his journey. He realised that tonight, for the first time in quite a while, he would have to find a place to sleep, and that could be difficult in poor country. And this was poor country. Increasingly scrubby vegetation and loamy soil, large tracts uncleared, houses and settlements well apart. As the sky clouded over and the temperature dropped Argus began to step out, but was unable to see any promising shelter. Finally, as the road ahead seemed to offer no prospects, he left it and pushed through the small trees to a hill, hoping to find a cave or an animal hole. But there was nothing ready-made there.

The afternoon darkened and the rain started to fall; he broke off some branches and combined them with dead wood to make a crude shelter, then crept inside and sat, knees up to his chest, watching the rain thicken into a steady downpour. His shelter did not do much of a job; it screened him from the small drops by catching them and gathering them into big drops, which then ran down the back of his neck. Or that was the way it seemed to him. He unrolled his pack and supped on some sandwiches and dried fruit the twins had given him.

His spirits were high enough, though as the last of the daylight melted he found it harder to maintain his morale. It was too early to sleep so he amused himself by trying to rearrange the shelter so less rain dripped through; then he tried to do some mental exercises. But he found the process dreary.

When it was too dark to see any more Argus lay down and tried to sleep. The rain slackened off but was still persistent. He knew that by going to sleep now he would almost certainly wake up again in the middle of the night but he decided to face that problem when he came to it. He slept fitfully, dreaming that he was floating down a river that flowed, not towards the ocean, but towards a vast inland lake. He woke up, then slept again, dreaming this time of birds who were being chased and caught by savage predators, who leapt up and tore the birds out of the sky. He woke, wanting to urinate and, after some minutes of reluctance and procrastination, crawled out and relieved himself on a patch of grass. He returned to the shelter and fell back into a stormy sleep, in which he was alternately chasing and being chased by bright lights which shone with an intensity that was alluring at times, at times threatening.

The next time he awoke he realised that he was not likely to get back to sleep again. He sat up and listened but the rain had stopped and the only sound to be heard was the drops of water that rolled and splashed through the trees. Argus moved to the door of the shelter and looked out. The cloud had disappeared. The sky glinted and glittered with a fresh intensity. Argus spent a little time sitting with his arms around his knees, gazing up at it.

After twenty minutes or so he was about to turn away when out of the corner of his eye he saw a light shooting quickly across the sky. He turned back and watched intently. The light moved among the stars at speed. It shone brightly as it traversed the heavens in an apparently fixed path. It took perhaps a minute to pass from Argus' view; the boy was transfixed for every second of that time, wondering what the light was and what it could portend. Long after it had disappeared he sat gazing at the spangled sky, hoping to see the light reappear, but he was disappointed. There was nothing to be seen but the everyday miracle of the stars in the night sky. At last, as the whitened sky in the east drew a gradual film over the purply blackness, he crawled back into the rough shelter and settled into a fitful new bout of sleep.

Chapter Sixteen

Following the road as it led up into the uncleared and unsettled areas, gaining height all the while, Argus saw ahead of him the figure of an old man on the road. The man was shabbily dressed but had a blanket-roll on his back much like Argus'. His head was bald on top but was ringed by long grey curls, which fell almost to his shoulders. Despite his venerable age he was walking quite rapidly, and Argus, who wanted to catch up with him, had to stride out vigorously to do so. When he reached him, he walked along with the man for quite a distance before either of them spoke. At last however the old man, without looking at Argus, said, 'I have one very good friend'.

'Oh yes?' said Argus politely, wondering if the old man were perhaps mad.

'Yes,' said the man, 'and here he is.' With a flourish, still not looking at the boy, he drew a large orange from his pocket and held it aloft. Argus was now sure that the man was mad. 'This is my very good friend,' said the man firmly, then he began ripping the peel from the orange and stuffing its flesh into his mouth, gulping it down voraciously. Argus thought of a number of facetious remarks he could make but wisely decided to make none of them. The old man finished the orange and spoke again.

'We're on a road to nowhere,' he said, 'and the only way we can get there is by eating our friends.' He danced a few steps, stirring up clouds of dust in the road. 'What do you want to know?' he asked. 'Any question you want to ask me. Go on, any question at all.' Argus was taken aback and did not know what to say. But the man was flitting on to another topic. 'There's nothing to say and no time to say it in,' he declared. 'There was a rabbit and an eagle, and then there was an eagle. Everything becomes the eagle in the end. But then, there's another way of looking at it. When there's a lot of light, you don't notice the dark. When there's a lot of dark you always notice the light. Now that's a strange thing. And so I dance and I sing.' He proceeded to do both, singing:

> A moth that flew to the moon,
> Discovered, and all too soon,
> The moon that burned so bright,
> Would never defeat the night.

'That's true,' said Argus, clutching in relief at what meaning he could recognise among the meanderings. 'Ah,' said the man, 'but is it as true as that rock? As true as this road? As true as the word "true" that comes out of your mouth? Now there's true and there's true and there's true, and that makes three, and that's three trues, all different and none of them lies. But that can't be right, because if there's a true there must be a lie. And each true must give way to the next true that comes along. And so,' he said, peering into the distance, 'I see our road coming to a junction, and you are going a different way from me, and we must part.'

'But,' said Argus, astonished, 'How do you know that I am going a different way?'

'Because whichever way you are going, I am going a different way,' said the man. 'Do you go the same way as a bird? As a kite? Do you know the way home? Is there air in your shoes and between your toes? I expect not. So fly in circles until you find the air.'

They had reached the crossroad and Argus stood, irresolute. The road they were on continued to the west, still a well-defined route. The road crossing it was a straggling track that hardly deserved to be called a road. The boy looked at the man. The man gazed away, deliberately not looking at the boy.

'Which way do you suggest?' Argus asked at last. The old man shrugged. 'One to the topmost,' he sang, 'and one to the coast.

> One that goes to earth,
> And another to a birth.
> The only one it cannot be
> Is the one that comes from the sea.

His dry crackled voice gave little comfort to Argus, who decided however that the way ahead looked boring, and so took the track to the left, to the south. The old man promptly took the one to the north and strode off along it, singing and muttering to himself. Argus shrugged and set out along his own chosen way.

The morning still had the cool freshness that characterises the early part of the day, before the sun has set about drying and heating the air and the ground. Argus walked and whistled. This was no time to be sour. He realised, with pleasure, that he was again noticing little things: the way a single blade of grass trembled as though palsied, though all around it was still; the way a creeper took such a tortuous path to the sun; the way one bird hopped on two feet while another walked, one foot in front of the other.

But the track soon began to dwindle into a path that was completely grassed over in places. A recent storm had crashed timber across it, so that Argus was now forced frequently into going over, under or around. After a while he began wondering what made him go on: not the rational thought that the track should lead to something. Perhaps the irrational reluctance to give up and return through what would be, with each step he took, stale territory. So he kept going, though with less and less of his earlier pleasure, and with less interest in the journey, as it took him through timbered country that was becoming depressingly uniform.

There was life, however, among the trees. A bird rose, almost at his feet, and flew swiftly away, with a harsh echoing cry. From bushes to his left a large black-and-white bird was hunted furiously by a small, aggressively maternal green and grey thrush. Detouring around yet another smashed and splintered tree Argus came face-to-face with a doe. He was enchanted. She gazed at him with troubled round eyes, big and brown, while the muscles under her coat trembled. She looked away, as if to say, 'This is not supposed to happen. What can we do?' Then, at some slight, half-imagined movement from Argus, she turned on the spot and fled, floundering through the broken branches in her hurry.

Argus went on. The country became more interesting: the forest was increasingly varied and the undergrowth thicker. The softness of the track and the moisture on the leaves indicated to the boy that he was passing into an area of greater rainfall. Presently the track crossed a creek. Argus slid over on a log but had to cast about for some moments to find the resumption of the path. It was obscured by fallen timber and marauding undergrowth.

More creek crossings followed, until inevitably Argus came to a substantial river. The water, although shallow, flowed rapidly. Looking up and down the river for a place to cross, Argus was struck by the beauty of the scene. Trees, tree-ferns and flowers crowded the banks on both sides. The further bank sloped steeply down to the water and vegetation covered every inch of it. Argus wondered at the inadequacy of a language that could provide only one word 'green' to describe the infinite variety of colours and shades on the slope.

The river itself was almost a continuous rapid: white water spumed among rocks, flurries of foam peered over huge boulders, providing just a hint of the churning below. Yet here and there were dark pools of extraordinary clearness. They reminded Argus of the eyes of the doe. He threw off his blanket-roll and approached one of the pools, gingerly stepping from rock to rock. A mottled dark-brown and green trout, sensing the boy's shadow, swerved with frantic speed out of the pool and was lost in a rapid.

Argus saw another huge pool further down the river, with two old white logs forming a bridge across the end of it. He clambered down to it. Through the clear water he could see every stone on the bottom, every aquatic insect, every grain of sand. Just beyond the centre of the pool was a dark and deep hole, its darkness a challenge to the clarity of the water; yet Argus could even see the rocks on its bottom. He pulled off his clothes and slung them across one of the white logs, took his customary glance down at his body to satisfy himself that he was growing properly, then dived in, his teeth gritted in what was both a smile of pleasure and a grimace of appalled anticipation of the coldness of the water.

Everything was disturbed by his dive. Huge ripples spread, meeting the banks like breaking waves. The mud and sand were stirred into dark clouds. Insects fled, and a piece of bark, lodged for a long time against a rock, was set free and swirled away downstream. Argus saw none of this but instead continued the disruption of this tiny universe by slapping the water with his hand, running in an arc around his body. He laughed delightedly, but the sound of his own voice made him self-conscious in a way that his body and its movement had not, and he made no further sound.

For five cold, exhilarating minutes he explored the pool, diving repeatedly, bringing up stones and throwing them away, even going to the bottom of the deep hole and bringing up a small red stone so beautiful that he wanted to keep it. He placed it next to his clothes on the log, and went on playing.

When he was too cold to continue he used the log as a fulcrum to swing himself around and out of the water, and sat on the edge, feeling the warmth of the sun dissolve his goose pimples. As he dressed, he noticed that the red stone had dried, but it had lost all its colour and lustre. Frustrated, he threw it back to the edge of the pool, where it sat dully among the other dry rocks.

At last, reluctantly, Argus continued on his way. The path dropped down now into a small valley and gave signs of an approaching destination. Ahead, the tops of trees were replaced by clear sky. But Argus was still surprised when he came into a fertile and grassy clearing; at its edge was a small hut, built of timber on a base of rocks. Argus walked steadily towards it. It bore all the traces of habitation: a couple of chairs with clothes draped over them were on a verandah and an open book lay on the ground. The door was ajar and a cat walked casually out as the boy approached.

Argus went to the doorway and knocked, peering with naïve curiosity into the dark interior. There was no answer, but he thought he heard a soft moan. He called out, 'Is anybody there?' The cat brushed past his legs as it strolled back into the hut, unconcerned at his presence. Argus called out again, 'Anyone home?'

There was a sound behind him and he turned, puzzled. It took him a moment to identify the noise as the wind rushing through the trees on the hill overlooking the clearing. He could see the trees bend as they were thrown around by the gusts; then the trees further down the hill started to toss as the wind advanced. It blew across the valley floor and Argus felt its cool strength rustle and buffet him.

He turned again to the doorway, this time certain that someone had moaned within the house. He called out, 'Excuse me, do you want me to come in?' and on receiving no answer went in anyway. The hut was small and untidy, but it was clean. There was a main room, which seemed to be the living and eating area, and two doorways which appeared to lead to smaller rooms. In the ceiling was a loft, reached by a ladder. A huge fireplace contained several large cooking pots.

Argus went to the left-hand doorway and looked in. He found himself staring into the face of a young girl who was lying on a low bed. Although her eyes were open, she seemed not to see him. His heart began to beat very quickly. He realised at once she was ill, and his mind flew back to the hut on the beach that he had visited with Temora.

Feeling awkward and embarrassed, very much a trespasser, Argus tiptoed to the edge of the bed. He had been slow to take in the details of the sickroom, but could see now that the girl was pregnant and in labour. He had a fierce desire to run, but fought it down. He said to her, 'Are you all right?'

She did not answer but seemed to refocus her eyes so that they were now resting on his face. Argus asked, 'Is there anyone else around? Is there anyone helping you?' Again there was no reply and the boy felt a little lost as to his next move. Finally, however, he went out to the main room again, poured a glass of water from a jug on the table, took that in and gave it to the girl. At first she seemed unable or unwilling to drink, but when he held it to her lips she showed more interest, and began at last to take small sips.

When she had finished Argus put the cup on the floor and said to the girl again, 'Have you got anyone to help you?' She looked at him now with eyes that showed understanding but she still did not answer.

Argus saw that the bottom half of the bed was soaked, and there were traces of blood on the wet sheets. He glanced around and was gratified to find piles of sheets, blankets and towels in a big box in a corner of the room. He fetched two towels and two sheets and carefully peeled the wet top sheet off the girl. His embarrassment and disconcertment at finding that she was naked from the waist down were quickly effaced by the sudden onset of her contractions.

Again a calm voice of sense inside Argus told him not to panic; he took the girl's hand and held it in his. It felt like a wet little bird that he had once found in a nest blown from a tree. She struggled and panted and cried out as the contractions gripped her. She squeezed his hand tightly and it was not until some moments after the contractions had ceased that Argus could get her to release her grip. He then dried her, as much as he was able and, afraid to try to pull out the bottom sheet, he instead raised her body a little and slipped dry towels in at several points.

Argus remembered something about boiling water and childbirth but wasn't sure what the boiling water was for. Besides, a new series of contractions was beginning and there was no time to do anything but hold on to her hand again. He realised that the birth of the baby must be imminent and no sooner did he have this thought than he saw the top of its head, an innocent pink island in a dark forest.

'Its head's showing,' he said to the girl in encouragement, but wasn't sure if she understood. Suddenly she began a new series of contractions that became almost continuous and she began talking in a low, hurried voice.

'Oh how it hurts, oh how it hurts. Push push push, how it hurts. Make me better, Jared.' Argus doubted that she knew what she was saying. She seemed to faint for a moment: her skin became pale and she fell back on the pillow again.

'Are you all right?' Argus asked.

'It was all dark,' she said. 'I saw a star, just one star.' Moments passed — Argus was not sure how many — with stronger and more sustained contractions, and the girl pushed harder and harder, until with a rush the baby slithered out.

Argus was not unaccustomed to birth. He had seen many animals come into the world, some dragged in painfully, others easily, like soft spring showers. But he thought that he had never seen anything quite as wonderful as this perfectly formed little human who lay between the legs of her panting mother and feebly beat the air with a tiny hand. He saw that the infant was a girl, but that seemed irrelevant. He watched in wonder, not daring to breathe. A golden glow of sunlight lay about the baby, so that her first blanket was one of freedom and warmth.

It was only the knowledge that this fragile creature depended on him that broke the spell the boy was under. He knew he had to tie and cut the cord and realised then why he should have boiled some water. He hurried back to the large first room again and found a knife in a saucepan of water in the fireplace. He returned to the baby and found her breathing healthily with little sobbing noises. The mother lay exhausted, her eyes closed.

Argus cut the cord rather clumsily and a little too far along, then nervously picked the baby up. He was astounded by her complex perfection. He placed her beside the mother, who opened her eyes and looked for the first time upon her daughter. An expression of wonder came into her face and Argus felt that at last her fever had broken and that she understood what was going on. She struggled to sit up. Argus supported her, then helped her to unbutton her shirt. As she took the baby to her breast and it began to suckle, the boy tactfully withdrew to the main room. A feeling of elation and lightness of heart took hold of him and shook him; he started to tidy the room in a noisy and boisterous fashion. When next he peeked into the bedroom, both mother and daughter were asleep.

Chapter Seventeen

Three days later Argus was still in the valley, but much had changed. The young mother, whose name, he had learned, was Adious, was recovering from her fever but was still weak and slept for many hours each day. The baby was thriving: she was a serene child who cried seldom and woke only at times that were convenient for everyone.

Of the three people who were sharing the hut, it was Argus who had to be the most active. He cooked, he cleaned, he cut wood. He learned how to change and wash the baby's garments. He prepared soups and nourishing meals for Adious. He tended the mob of sheep that seemed to be the focus of the farm's existence. He carried water, fed the cat, and cleared the gutters and drains after each of the frequent storms that swept through the little valley. The third room in the cottage, which gave evidence of having been prepared with loving care for the baby's coming, was Argus' temporary bedroom; he made a bed by stuffing a mattress cover with bracken, and fell exhausted on to it every night.

His conversations with Adious began to acquire more form. At first she had accepted his presence unquestioningly, but as her health improved she began to show more curiosity. He judged her to be about seventeen; she was a stunningly attractive black-haired girl with dark haunting eyes. She watched him as he scrubbed her floor and asked: 'Who are you? Someone sent, to be my guardian? Where do you come from?' Her voice had a slightly foreign flavour; Argus found it exotic and attractive. He leaned back on his heels and laughed.

'My name's Argus. I just happened to take this path, and I just happened to keep following it,' he said, but at the same time he wondered if indeed it had been chance. 'Then I found this valley and this hut, and there you were, looking like you needed some help. Do you remember much about it? I mean, about giving birth and so on?'

'No,' she answered. 'But I remember that every time I felt terrible, you were there, and you were kind and gentle. How long have you been here?'

'Nearly three days,' Argus said, but at this she became distressed, and started up on her pillow.

'Three days!' she cried, 'Where's Jared?'

'Who's Jared?' Argus asked, alarmed at her sudden fear. 'You called out his name when you were having the baby, but there's been nobody here but me.'

'Jared's my husband,' she said, sinking back onto the bed. 'Something must have happened to him. He left when I went into labour, to fetch the midwife. She's only a day's journey from here. Something has happened to him.'

Argus stood up. 'Which way would he have gone?' he asked.

'There's only one way out of this valley,' she said. Argus assumed it was the same way he came.

He arranged some food for Adious, changed the baby again and set out along the track. He walked quickly.

But he did not have far to travel. After less than an hour he heard voices approaching, so he stopped and waited. Around a bend in the track came a group of men, sombrely dressed, carrying a stretcher. After a moment Argus saw that the face of the body on the stretcher was covered, signifying death. The men stopped when they saw him.

'Who are you?' asked one of them, an unshaven man of perhaps forty, with the weatherbeaten face and rough hands of a farmer.

'I've been helping, in the valley,' Argus explained falteringly, suddenly feeling very young again. 'The girl had a baby, and she was sick.' The men looked at each other in despair.

'Ah, she's had it already,' one said, 'and my wife was not there.' They put down the stretcher and crowded around, asking questions.

'How is she?' 'How is the baby?' 'Wasn't she worried about her husband?' 'How long have you been there?' Argus answered as many questions as he could, then thought it was time to ask one of his own.

'Is that her husband. Is that Jared?' he asked. 'What happened to him?'

The men suddenly fell silent, and stood back again. Finally the first man spoke: 'We found him under a fallen tree,' he said. 'There was a storm . . . many trees came down.'

Argus sat down as the implications of this death began to dawn on him. The men adopted various positions, leaning against trees, sitting on the ground. Argus thought, 'On her own . . . a new baby . . . she's still not even able to stand.' The tragedy of it all welled up in his stomach and came into his throat. He covered his eyes with his hands. 'A death and a birth,' he thought.

The men stirred, picked up the stretcher and began the last phase of their procession. Argus followed disconsolately.

The following days marked Argus forever. There was the grief of a girl whom he no longer thought of as beautiful but rather as a fascinating and unpredictable person. A solemn burial under a grey sky, the figures of the mourners etched against the dun background. A baby named Jessie, who gripped Argus' finger in her little hand, and who fell asleep comfortably in his arms as he rocked her. A desperate ride through the night for help when it appeared that the baby had become seriously ill. The inexpressible relief and joy when he found, upon his return, that the illness had been nothing more than a stomach upset...

A week passed, and another, and another. Neither Adious nor Argus mentioned the possibility of his leaving. Each day he busied himself with work both indoors and outdoors, improving the hut and the farm. He carried out short-term jobs and long-term jobs. He rehung a dragging door and sowed wheat and oats. 'This valley's too wet for sheep,' he said to Adious that night. She smiled, for the first time since the burial. 'Yes,' she admitted, 'Jared was no farmer.'

Her story slowly emerged. She had been born at sea, the daughter of a ship's captain who travelled with his wife. She had seen many wild and tranquil sights. As the years went on her mother tended to stay at home, caring for a family that had grown to five children — Adious and two sets of twins. When Adious was older she began to travel once more with her father on his trading voyages. On one such trip she fell in love with a new member of the crew, Jared. They had married less than a year ago, and had come to the valley to learn farming. She was just seventeen years old.

During the day she and Argus would work separately or together, but they found time to play too. On hot days they swam; on cooler days they took long walks and explored the tangled forests that surrounded the valley. The baby would ride in a pouch on her mother's back. In the evenings they ate together at the rough timber table, while Jessie slept in a basket on the floor beside them. Adious loved to hear Argus read, so after dinner most nights he would read aloud from one of the few books in the meagre hut's poor collection. She particularly loved to hear stories of the sea, but would get passionately angry at any inaccuracies in them.

After a few months they began to sleep together. It happened in an almost casual way, without planning and without drama, although both of them had considered the possibility many times. One night as they began to ease towards their respective rooms Argus lingered a little, and Adious took him by the hand and led him to her room. He expected her to be wild in bed, and on the second night she was, but that first time she was slow and gentle, almost dreamy. Argus worried that she might be remembering Jared, but he tried to put the thought out of his mind.

Other changes came about. Jessie began to show much joy when Argus returned to the hut after a day's work. Argus looked forward to these moments in a way that made him realise how deeply bonded they had become since their first tentative contact on that wet and threatening afternoon so many months before.

Argus was changing. He was growing taller at a disconcertingly rapid rate. He was becoming stronger across the chest and developing muscles in his arms and legs. His body hair was spreading; he tried to ignore with dignity Adious' teasing, and was secretly proud that he had to borrow Jared's razor more and more often.

They did not have many visitors in the valley. None came by chance and few by design. The nearest farmers and their wives took it in turn to make formal visits after Jared's death, to pay their respects to the young widow. They showed no concern at the unconventional presence of Argus, but watched him closely, as if to assess his capabilities. Apparently satisfied by what they saw the men each took him solemnly aside and outlined the jobs that needed doing around the farm. They assumed that he was adept at physical labour, but in fact Adious was probably stronger than he was. As the baby grew a few months older, Adious was able to do more outdoors work.

The days shortened and winter began to close its grim hand around the valley — forcing them to concentrate on two major tasks: clearing another section of the valley for crops and building up huge stocks of firewood. They extended the vegetable garden behind the hut and covered it with straw as protection against frost. It would be a hard winter and they trained their stomachs by restricting themselves to two meals a day.

Argus left the valley only once, to take wheat and vegetables to a small trading centre called Fesquina, which was nearly a full day's journey from their sheltered home. He used a handcart, which Jared had brought into the valley when he and his bride had first arrived there. It was not easy to tow the laden cart over the rough walking tracks, and Argus was exhausted by the time he arrived.

Most of the bartering was over for the day so the boy had to be patient and endure a cold sleep under a tree before trading his stock. He used the money he made to buy essentials he and Adious had agreed they needed. These included salt and sugar, smoked fish, tools, needles and thread, oil, and some more books.

From the moment he had left the valley Argus missed the company of Adious and Jessie. He felt responsible for them. He set a quick pace on the trip home and the cart bounced crabbily behind him. His only indulgence was to stop at a tree that was beautifully encrusted with a vine bearing late autumn flowers, fragrant yellow and green. Argus picked armfuls of creeper and filled the cart with them: these, and an old silver ring that he had bought in Fesquina, were the presents he brought home to Adious.

Chapter Eighteen

The two young people never tired of each other's company. Through the long winter Argus and Adious delighted in exploring each other, physically and spiritually. Yet Argus knew that there were dark depths of Adious that would never be plumbed, not by him, not by anyone, not even by Adious herself. She was a poem, a painting, the coals of a fire. She was a night of stars and a moody river. For her part Adious was seduced by the brown-eyed boy who had come from nowhere. She remembered little of the fever-filled days that had seen Jessie brought out of her body. She had made assumptions about him in those early days but they all proved fallacious.

At first she thought of him as just a boy who was helping her through her pain and illness. Later, as she silently watched him, she had decided that he was a farmboy, good at practicalities, good with his hands. But it was those same hands that brought her to the realisation that there was something more to him. The hands that had lifted her and supported her were firm and steady, but also gentle. There was a maturity about them that she had not expected from one who looked so young. As they began to talk she was surprised by the intelligence of his quiet comments, and she began to recognise the laughing liveliness in his eyes. When, much later, they made love, it was again his hands that she remembered afterwards. He had the hands of a ploughboy but he used them like an artist.

Argus had a perceptiveness that at times threw Adious into a confusion of thought and led her to reorganise large areas of her mind. He seemed to see patterns different from those other people saw. He jumped across constraints of language and thinking. One night, when he sliced some pumpkin for the evening meal, he carved each slice, with a few deft twists of his knife, into the shape of a butterfly and announced that the tea-time vegetable would be steamed butterflies. Where Adious saw a snail that threatened the vegetables, Argus saw its silver path and identified it as a mirror of the constellations in the sky. When frantic ants spilled from a burning log in the fireplace he would grab the log with a piece of sacking that he kept for the purpose and race outside with it. He hated to kill anything, or even to contribute to the death of anything, except the fish they needed for their own food supplies. In consequence there was soon a pile of half-burnt logs outside the door, and cobwebs in all the corners of the hut.

Argus was fascinated by the endless paradoxes that he saw around him. In particular he was interested in the contradictions between apparent and real freedom. He watched the clouds, with their seemingly random movement through the heavens. Yet he knew they were really at the mercy of the wind. The river was defined and limited by its own banks, and the birds, whose effortless flights symbolised freedom, were on the end of an intangible cord that led to their nests and their mates and their young.

For the first time Argus became fully aware of the paradox of his own situation and started to understand the nature of his parents' commitment to their farm and to their son. There were days when he became giddy with homesickness, and on those days he would spend hours cradling Jessie in his arms and singing softly to her.

Argus began to write poems, especially on the cold winter evenings in front of the fire. He did not know how the urge to write them had come upon him, nor did he know whence the poems came. He was writing them before he really knew that it was happening. It was some weeks before he wondered how and when he had begun. He was reminded of the way in which he had gradually eased into puberty: one day he had realised that hair had been growing on his body for a while, but he could not remember when it had started. He wrote:

> Skin like rain, but more.
> Eyes like clouds, but more.
> Hair like nightfall.
>
> The rest is you.

After a dream, he wrote:

> Rain slips
> Across the glass
> In endless downpour.
> It drums against the door
> When winter falls.
>
> Birds beat
> Their lonely way

Against the clouds, on course.
Towards an unknown source
When winter falls.

We sit
And laugh and talk,
Listen to the wind squalls.
The building creaks and calls
When winter falls.

He was aware that he did not always understand what
he had written. And Adious, although she was stirred and
moved by the poems, was too wise to ask him what they
meant.
He wrote:

your yellow yearning fall across the sun

did you plummet, cold hard stone
or were we with you
so you were held?

flying not falling.

He wrote a love poem to Adious and gave it to her on
a grey and lifeless night, when they were sick of each other
and of the hard winter in the valley. She read it by the
fire as the coals burned a second time in her glowing face:

Loving you is all I want to be,
There is, you see, no other world but this,
The one implanted lightly by your kiss.

Loving you is all I want to say.
No other way: let one be lost in two.
I'm happy just to live my life in you.

Loving you is how it all began,
My guardian. And that's the mystery:
How ties that bound were ties that set me free.

All I want to be is loving you.
A world for two, where nothing else is known
And all the rest is left to sleep alone.

Chapter Nineteen

When Spring came Argus and Adious were fit but lean and hungry. Jessie was the plumpest of the three of them, a serene and dreamy baby who rarely cried but chortled and kicked her little legs at the daily pleasures of life in the valley. But her life there was due to be interrupted. Argus had decided to resume his journey, to make towards his parents' home and bring his quest to a finish. Adious and Jessie were to travel with him as far as Conroy, a large town where Adious' aunt lived, not far from Random. At a later date they would either come on and join Argus in Random, or he would pick them up and the three of them would return to the valley, to take up more permanent residence there.

Argus went away for two days to negotiate with neighbouring farmers for the care of the sheep and the harvesting of their crops and vegetables. Argus and Adious would take little with them, as the handcart was too slow and awkward to tow. So the preparation for the trip did not take long. In the event, though, it was several weeks before they actually left: the weather remained unstable and both were a little reluctant to leave their safe and secure hut for the perils of the road. Argus in particular was somewhat perplexed how he would explain a wife and child — which, for all practical purposes Adious and Jessie were — to his parents.

Before they left Adious made a last sad pilgrimage to Jared's grave, laying on it the first wild rosebuds of the Spring. She stayed there some hours, and when she returned her mood was one of melancholy. Argus kept his distance and allowed her time to shed her sadness gradually.

The journey began. Argus stepped out with a fine vigour, sad to be leaving the valley, but excited to be on the road again, with fresh sights in the offing. It took him only a few moments to realise, however, that this was going to be a very different kind of walking. Despite the extra weight he carried he was too fast for Adious, who had Jessie in a pouch on her back. It took Argus several days to adjust, and even then there were times when he was so frustrated that he had to run ahead, or take an extravagant detour through a paddock.

The weather was good, but erratic, and they slept under bridges the first few nights because of threatening clouds. Jessie was fascinated by the whole exercise and gazed in speechless astonishment at each fresh sight they came upon. She was able to sit up comfortably now, and could even move around a little. It was one of Argus' constant delights to be able to bring little oddities to her from the fields and forests — objects that she could play with or eat or both. He brought her flowers and coloured stones, feathers and insects. If he could have brought her a wisp of mist from a cloud, he would have. The two of them, the young man and the baby, were deeply in love with each other.

After three days' walking they camped by a stream in a place so pleasant that they decided to stay there a full day. Adious was not used to doing so much walking and was developing blisters on both feet. They spent most of the day sleeping, eating blackberries and looking for birds' eggs, which were there in abundance. Around mid-afternoon, Argus' attention was caught by a deep silence that suddenly seemed to engulf the whole clearing. He looked across at where Jessie slept in the sun. Curled up snugly next to her, nestled into the warmth of her body, was a snake about as long as Argus was tall. It was black and thick and menacing even in its somnolence.

Argus' heart began to race. Moisture broke out on his palms at the same time as it drained away from his mouth. He needed no time to assess the dilemma. Indeed he seemed never to have thought so coolly and clearly. If he approached the snake, or made any movement to startle it, it was likely to bite Jessie. Yet if he waited too long, Jessie would wake up, and would kick about or cry out, which would also invite an attack. And then there was the further complication of Adious who was somewhere upstream. She might come back at any moment and unwittingly provoke the snake.

For five long minutes Argus sat and sweated. Several times the baby stirred and moved. Several times the snake restlessly rearranged its coils. In that short time Argus came to appreciate another of the grim complexities of life: the fact that no-one can refuse to be involved. Not to act is as deliberate as the decision to act. A small bird flew suddenly out of a thicket of blackberries and the snake lifted its sleepy head and followed the flight of the bird with vague interest. This reaction gave Argus an idea.

What if he could make enough of a disturbance to make the snake uneasy, but not enough to panic it? He thought he could hear Adious singing to herself in the distance, and the danger posed by her possible approach forced him to act quickly. He picked up a stone and threw it against some rocks on the other side of the stream. The clatter it made caused the snake to raise its head sharply. Argus waited a minute and threw another stone in about the same place. The snake stirred and uncoiled half of its length. Argus threw a third stone but it fell in grass and made no sound. Just then Adious called out, 'Argus! Argus!' The snake, for the first time, separated itself from the baby's body. Argus threw another stone and the snake glided off a few feet. Argus leapt out of cover at it and the snake, startled, slithered quickly away and was gone, like black lightning in the grass.

The boy bent over and put his hands on his knees. He shook uncontrollably for a few seconds. But Jessie was awake now, and gurgling, and he could hear Adious coming towards their clearing. As so often, the ordinary and the commonplace filled the available space, and there was no time to dwell on the heroic. He picked up the baby and went to meet her mother.

Chapter Twenty

Their slow journey took them along the top of a steep escarpment, giving spectacular views for many miles. Under gigantic skies swept with vast clouds the two small specks moved steadily westwards. The weather had held, and they were all brown and healthy. Jessie's lively eyes were testimony to their lifestyle. Water, soaking from the ground in numerous green crevices, was plentiful. In the distance the sun gleamed on lakes and dams scattered like mirrors across the countryside. A dreamy brown river, lined with trees, dawdled away from them in ever-widening bends.

It had been three days since they had seen any other people — two women on horses, riding hard, as though on an urgent errand. Argus and Adious had stood politely aside on the narrow track but had received neither acknowledgement nor thanks for their gesture.

Argus and Adious spent many hours now walking in companionable silence. They no longer needed words to express the awe they felt as a huge eagle lifted from the heath near them and flapped away, nor to express their amusement as two birds diving for a piece of apple narrowly avoided a head-on collision. They spent much of their time pulling faces and poking out tongues at Jessie, who gurgled with endless delight at these obliging humans who nonetheless always grew tired of the game before she did.

At night, beside the fire that was burning quietly down into coals, Argus wondered again at the fascination that glowing coals had for all men and women. Had life itself been born in molten rock and fire, and did man somewhere have a dim memory of this? Was it the duality of fire, its power to destroy and its power to give comfort, that fascinated people, who instinctively recognised the same duality in themselves? Was man afraid of fire? The fire burned with its greatest intensity as it neared the end of its life. That was when its heat was at its utmost, when it was at its most alluring. The young fire that burned raw gave little heat and held little interest.

Argus felt frustrated again at the inadequacy of his language which held no words to describe the colour of fire. Yellow, orange, red: they were the words most commonly used, but they were wrong. They failed to evoke the smouldering power of these glowing coals.

Perhaps it was the panther-like quality of the fire that held men in its thrall. Controlled, circumscribed, secured, this fire was kept within its bounds by a few rocks and by the boy's watchful supervision. Yet, like the panther on a chain, the restraint of the fire was an illusion. A moment's carelessness, the intervention of some other force, like wind, and the fire would snap its chain. Raging and foaming, it would leap at the throat of a dead tree, rip and tear through the grass of the plateau, and gorge itself in a savage gloating feast on the bodies of every creature in its domain.

Adious, who had been washing herself in a nearby spring, walked back into the light of the fire. She had not bothered to dress again, having always been much less self-conscious about her body than Argus. Her lithe and feline beauty struck Argus anew with its force. Her dark skin gleamed in the firelight, but her black springing curls absorbed the light like some kind of sombre night-time mystery. Argus took a piece of charcoal from the edge of the fire and with strong firm lines began to draw her on a slab of rock that had been at his back. He had never drawn much, and had never been very good at it, but now the lines flowed, like runnels of velvet. The charcoal was still warm in his hand as he drew.

Adious sat by the fire, eating an orange, not aware of what Argus was doing. She had torn the orange open and was biting into it, unconcerned about the spraying and spilling down her chin. Argus could not draw that, so he drew her at rest, lying on her side, a hand supporting her head. Yet it was impossible to portray her as relaxed; there was no mistaking the ripple of the muscles under her gleaming skin.

Finishing the orange, Adious rolled over, stood up and came to see what he was doing. She laughed, and became self-conscious.

'Don't.'

'What?'

'You've made me look like an animal.'

Argus laughed and continued to draw, but he too had become self-conscious, and the lines now would not come out; they formed clumsy shapes.

'Oh, don't!' Adious said again, grabbing at the stick of charcoal to stop him. Argus fought back and in a moment they were locked in a fierce wordless struggle, melded together in sudden heat. Although they were both snuffling and giggling Argus felt that there was something acrid in the fight. He sensed from the strength of Adious' grip that she felt the same. They rolled in the dust, first Argus on top, then Adious. Adious sat on top of him and laughed down into his face. He laughed back, then did a quick roll that upset her and reversed the positions. It was a struggle, a battle, but for what? Argus did not know, but he panted and growled at her, determined to win. She twisted and kicked and they were lying side by side in the warm ashes at the edge of the fire, the girl's skin reflecting the light like copper. They rested for a moment, locked together, then the scuffle began again. But as it did so the tension was cracked by a thin wail from Jessie, who had awoken and was demanding attention.

'You go,' said Adious.

'You go,' said Argus.

'No it's your turn.'

'Go on.'

'You go.'

'You look after Jessie,' said Adious, 'and I'll get some wood for the fire.'

'All right,' said Argus, after a moment's thought.

But later that night, as he lay in peace beside Adious, looking up at the burning stars, he wondered at the tension that had flickered so quickly and been resolved so quickly. Their friendship had a sharp edge that he had come to like.

Chapter Twenty-One

Argus and Adious continued on their way under a cloudless sky. The view was changing; they had left behind the cultivated flatlands that stretched out from the foothills below, and now wended their way above dense and wild country. At dusk they watched as a thousand or more small black birds plunged from trees at the top of the escarpment to their roosting places in the forest below. A litter of baby foxes, each with beautifully long flared brushes, scattered at their approach and ran, one of them with something furry held in his mouth. A mob of horses, feeding on the rough grass, moved uneasily as the small cavalcade went past, and stood watching until the travellers were out of sight.

Walking became difficult at times, over sharp loose rocks. For three days and three nights they pressed doggedly on above the great brooding cliffs and slashing gullies. On the fourth day they began to emerge into populated areas again, and to drop down from the ridgeline.

The country they were now in was only semi-cleared and lightly settled. There were many dark patches of forest which the track wound through tentatively. Farming in these regions seemed a desultory affair: the land had not by any means surrendered to the people. The people merely camped at its edges and made shabby incursions into the wilder parts. There were plenty of tubers to be dug out of the ground for food — some of them of a type that neither Argus nor Adious had seen before. Argus worked for a day on a small farm in exchange for fruit, but found his employer to be surly and ungrateful. Hurt by his attitude, Argus finished early and took his payment in an equally surly way.

'Moods are contagious, personalities are contagious, everything's contagious,' Adious said to him that night as they lay together in their blankets, with Jessie dribbling on a piece of cord nearby.

'Maybe,' Argus said. 'Let's move on fast tomorrow. I don't like this area. It was good up on the escarpment. I liked being up there.' He lay back with his arms behind his head and looked up at the sky, but the dark trees obscured most of the stars and denied him one of his favourite night-time occupations. There was a rustle in the branches though and he thought he could see a small face and a pair of little black eyes gleaming down at him.

'What is it?' Adious asked.

'I don't know . . . something furry and small,' said Argus, peering intently upwards. He could see a long tail wrapped around a branch.

'I'll find out,' he said and with a sudden impulse of energy leapt out of the blankets and swung up into the lower foliage.

'Careful!' Adious called out, torn between laughter and anxiety. But Argus was now climbing confidently. Even Jessie had stopped playing and was staring up into the tree but all that could be seen was an occasional glimpse of the boy as he gained height rapidly. He could see the animal more clearly but then realised that there was more than one. In fact there seemed to be a treeful of them. But they showed no awareness of his presence. He was now three-quarters of the way up the tree and with reckless disregard for the consequences began to shake the upper branches vigorously. The animals, of a type unknown to him, reacted with varying degrees of alarm. Several ran out to perilous positions among the buds and tips but most stayed around the trunk. Argus moved up to another foothold and a certain amount of panic set in. At last one of them ran straight down the trunk and down Argus' back and leg, treating him as part of the tree in its headlong dash to safety. Argus chortled, swung around the tree and laughed.

'What's happening?' Adious laughed up at him.

'They're running all over me!' he yelled. 'And they've got claws!' Several more followed their leader down. As the last one swarmed down the boy's back he gave a quick lurch of his shoulders and the little creature was flung through the air, tumbling and turning in a shower of leaves. Then he landed on a more substantial branch and swung his tail around it in a firm grip. He shook himself and ran off along the branch into the dark sanctuary of the foliage.

Argus, his fun finished, came down reluctantly. It was one of the few times that he missed the company of a boy his own age. He was aware that most of his friends had been adults, like Mayon, or girls, like Temora and Adious. He had gained much from these friendships. In fact he was wise enough to recognise that through them he had gained in ways that placed him far ahead of most of his peers. Yet he would have liked someone to wrestle and roll around with, someone who could race him up a tree or outswim him across a dam. Instead he contented himself with tickling Jessie and rolling her backwards and forwards across her blanket — thus arousing the wrath of Adious, who had been assiduously lulling the child to sleep.

Argus was still restless but with no outlet for his energy he was forced to crawl sulkily back under his blankets, while Adious, still grumbling, came in beside him. It was only a few minutes before she was asleep: Argus watched the rise and fall of the blanket over her and the stillness of her dark cheeks. He sighed and looked up at the tree again, but could see no sign of life.

An hour or two passed. Argus lightly drifted in and out of sleep but was never sure whether he was asleep or awake. Then a branch cracked in the darkness and he was sure that he was awake. He lay still, his heart pounding. He had heard many sounds during many nights in many strange places but there was something deliberate and watchful about this sound that set it apart. This was danger. Beside him Adious stirred a little and murmured something about 'hurting, hurting'. Argus wished he could quieten her but realised that any attempt to do so was likely to cause her to make even more noise. He lightly pushed the blankets aside and waited. Suddenly the stillness of the night was torn apart, so quickly and dramatically that he was made helpless by shock.

He did not know where to start. Things were happening everywhere. There were dark shapes rushing at him, a wave of them. They were big and, although he was ready to believe that they were evil apparitions, his rational mind told him that they were men. He flinched from the expected attack but it did not come. Just as they appeared to be about to fall on him they paused, grabbed at something on the ground and swept it up. For a moment they seemed hesitant, caught as a wave can sometimes be caught at the moment of its breaking. Then, as Argus began to struggle to his feet and Adious beside him began to stir into wakefulness, the men faded back into the darkness. Argus felt some kind of relief, as he registered the possibility that he might not be attacked. He was on his feet now, peering after them. Assuming they had stolen some of their few possessions, he cast around on the ground. It took him another infinitely slow moment to realise what they had taken.

'What's happening?' Adious asked, rubbing her eyes.

'They've taken Jessie,' Argus shouted, about to lunge out after them but realising in frustration that he would have to put shoes on first. That took another maddening moment. Adious was making sounds of horror. Then she was stumbling past him, pulling on her boots as she ran.

'Take the path,' Argus gasped. 'I think they went through the trees, so we might gain on them.' He plunged forwards, behind Adious, who was the only other person he could see or hear. He was too desperate to feel anything. He caught up with Adious and they ran silently on together, for three or four minutes. Then they paused to listen. There was nothing. Then, perhaps, for a moment, there was something. A thump, quite a way to the right, and in front of them. They ran towards it and found a narrow animal track. Following it they came to an old fence and swung themselves heavily over it. Argus landed on all fours with a crumpling noise that sounded like the one they had heard just a few moments before. He was up and running again, travelling more easily now that the initial shock was over. In the distance, through the dark trees, he imagined he saw the glimmer of a lantern, but it was gone again quickly and he was not sure. As he ran on he began thinking of the terror that Jessie must be experiencing, and that forced him to find more speed and stamina. In front of him, grim and silent, ran the mother. Argus wondered as he went what he would do if and when he caught up with the attackers.

Sick fear churned in his stomach, as if he had eaten a mixture of porridge and rotting fruit. He could hear Adious' breath start to come hard, louder, and with a pumping sound. He put his head down and ploughed on. His head began to roll from side to side and his arms were chopping down harder. A bird suddenly started up out of the dense dark grass beside the track, with a clatter of wings and a hollow series of short cries.

Unexpectedly they came to a road which was wide and well-made. They paused irresolute for a moment and then, without discussion, turned to the right and ran steadily along it. The change in surface and surroundings gave them a new burst of energy, which sustained them for perhaps twenty minutes.

The time came, however, when mental willpower was simply not enough. The body began to give out, in ways that could not be governed by the mind. The muscles at the backs of their legs contracted, and their steps became shorter and shorter. Cramps tore at their tortured limbs. Sweat poured down Argus' face, and the constant flow of salt into his mouth made him feel sick. It ran into his eyes too, stinging them. He at last slowed to a walk, hating himself for his weakness, but Adious seemed glad of the excuse to stop running; they walked along quickly for a few minutes, hands on hips, gasping at the grudging air. Finally Adious stopped completely.

'This is useless,' she said. 'We don't even know if we're going the right way.'

'What do we do then?' Argus asked miserably. There was no answer and he started trying to think objectively, to analyse the situation and work out the best strategy. Panic kept threatening to gum up his mind and he had to fight hard to muster some self-control.

'It'll be light in a few hours,' he said at last, as calmly as possible. 'We'd be better to rest and wait till then. We'll be able to see, and we'll still have some energy left. Besides, they'll have to rest too, unless they've got horses, and if they've got horses they'll already be over the hills and far away.'

They sagged onto the ground under a large tree and waited. It took some hours and they both dozed a little, although they would scarcely have thought it possible they could sleep. When it was light enough to distinguish the shapes of the trees from the grey sky, they rose without need of words, and began to move stiffly on their way. They walked a little, jogged a little, walked a little. Daylight continued to colour in the day. They followed the same road, for there seemed nothing else to do.

After about an hour they saw a man walking in the same direction as themselves. Carrying a spade and a bucket, he was clearly on his way to work. They ran up behind him, but he did not turn around until they were level with him, and even then he showed little interest, merely glancing at them.

'Have you seen anyone with a little child?' Argus begged. 'A baby girl, dark hair, dark eyes?' The man just kept walking, saying nothing, so that both Argus and Adious thought that he had not heard the question and might perhaps be deaf. But as they were about to speak again the man looked at them more searchingly. There was something surly about his expression and Argus inwardly quailed. But as the man took in their grimy, streaked faces and their desperate appearance, his face softened a little. He looked away and walked on but finally, after a fashion, answered their question.

'You're on the right road,' he said gruffly.

Argus was about to ask more questions but Adious, perhaps sensing that they would get no more information here, was already running away. The boy quickly followed.

The morning took some time to settle into the pattern of weather that it would maintain for the rest of the day: cloudy and humid, white cloud becoming grey. Argus sweated, and struggled to keep going. As the morning wore on they both abandoned any attempt to run. Not knowing where they were going or what they were looking for they nevertheless could see no alternative to following the road.

Late in the morning they passed two girls sitting on a gate but the girls looked contemptuously at them and ignored their questions. The only relief came when they found a long fence overgrown with a vine that seemed to be some kind of wild tomato; it was heavily laden with fruit and the two ate ravenously. The vivid red tomatoes were the only things in the landscape that were growing strongly. Everything else was straggly and sour.

As they left the spot Adious found a handkerchief on

147

the ground that she recognised at once as one that she had made for Jessie.

The discovery came at a crucial time. Somehow they had both ceased to understand the reality of what they were doing, of what was happening. The panic had never left them but it was becoming harder to remember that a successful end to the search would mean a reunion with Jessie. The frantic activity of the chase was obscuring its purpose. With a tangible clue in their hands they were infused with new energy and the search became focused again.

Quite late in the afternoon they came to a junction: not a true junction, because the road they were on was large and well-defined, whereas the track that joined it from the north-west was little-used. They had passed other such junctions before and ignored them, but this time for some reason they felt drawn to the narrow path, and stopped.

'This way?' Argus asked, raising his eyebrows. Adious nodded, and they took the path without any attempt to discuss their reasons. They jogged at a steady pace but with increasing nervousness as their field of vision decreased.

The track wound upwards for a long time. An occasional sob of weariness escaped Argus' throat now, despite his best efforts to control himself. He was sweaty, staggering, scorched with heat and hunger. Ahead of him, grimly determined, was Adious, growing more morose with every passing hour. Argus spared a thought for whoever had taken Jessie, wondering how they would cope with the vengeful mother. He felt fortified by the knowledge that she was with him.

Towards dusk they came to a hillock. Suddenly Adious stopped; so suddenly in fact that Argus ran into her back. It took only a moment for him to realise what had caught her attention: a thin trail of white smoke straggled up into the air, a steady wisp. They both stood and watched it for a moment, then moved on, keeping lower to the ground, and separating from each other a little. They nestled up to a ridge of granite-like rock that crocodiled along the top of the knoll.

The smoke came from a small fire that had just been lit. A lean dark boy, perhaps seventeen years old, was crouched over the fire, feeding it with pine-cones. Three or four men were sitting under trees around the clearing. A piece of canvas was slung between some trees, and under it sat two shabbily dressed women, scrawny and impassive. Beside them, apparently asleep, lay Jessie.

Argus was startled to feel Adious' hand grip his arm and to hear a low growl of rage rumble from her throat. Argus had sensed as the day had progressed that he and Adious were drawing apart: intent upon the desperate search for her daughter she had seemed almost to forget his existence. And this had reminded him, for the first time in months, that he was not Jessie's real father. Theirs were not bonds of blood, even though his links with this small family seemed to him to be unbreakable. Thus it was that Adious' grip on his arm was a welcome one. Amongst other things, it was saying to him, 'Hold me back. Restrain me. Don't let me do anything hot-headed.' She was telling him she was aware of Argus' presence and that he was necessary to her.

They lay together for some time watching while darkness submerged the world. The people they were watching, perhaps thinking they had placed themselves beyond the risk of pursuit, seemed to have no plans to move on for the evening. Jessie awoke and cried. Her voice was a thin wail slipping through the air like smoke from the fire. One of the women breast-fed her, and Argus was awed at the black rage that filled Adious' face at the sight. But once the feeding was over, the adults showed no further interest in the baby. Jessie lay still on the cloth that had been placed under her, though her eyes stayed open.

As they watched, Argus tried to formulate an ingenious plan to rescue the child. All he could think of, however, was the obvious: to slip in quietly when it was dark and carry Jessie away without causing any disturbance. But he felt that this plan was too vague, contained too many chances of going wrong. Whatever they did had to be foolproof, surely — the risks to Jessie were too great. At the back of his mind was the fear — or was it knowledge? — that there might be no foolproof plan. There were times when the safety, even the life itself, of every child hung in the balance. There were no guarantees, never had been, that every child would reach adult life easily or comfortably. The short life of Argus' own sister was evidence of that.

There was little light left in the sky. Argus and Adious, the two watchers, slid back a short distance to discuss their approach. Could one of them create a diversion while the other crept up? Could they use force, with so many adults against them? Was some kind of bluff possible? They tried to assess each idea calmly, even as the suggestions grew wilder. Set fire to the canvas, to create a barrier between Jessie and the people? Throw sand in their eyes? Find a good long creeper and come swinging down out of the trees?

By now it was dark. The small fire shed just a little light, enough for them to see that the people were sitting around the fire, apparently unconcerned about the baby. They could only assume that she was still under the canvas. They began to realise that there might be no brilliant solutions, that surprise and their own determination would be their only assets. They considered waiting until everyone had gone to sleep, but rejected the idea, in case they went to sleep under the canvas beside Jessie. But Argus did recollect one thing that might help them: the ground on which the people were camped was all earth and grass. There was no sign of any rocks. Yet the ridge that they were hiding behind was riddled with stones. He gathered ten or so, each about the size of his fist, and made a sling out of his shirt to carry them.

And so the plan had to be this: they would creep up from the undefended side and get as close as they could. When they were heard, as they undoubtedly would be, they would rush and hope. They agreed to make no human sounds, so that the assault might have as much mystery as possible. Adious would grab Jessie and Argus would hurl the rocks. If separated they would meet again at the intersection of the little track with the road.

It took them some twenty minutes to work their way around to a point that would bring them in at about the right place. Choked with fear and excitement, they began to worm forward. To Argus, every clatter and rustle that Adious made sounded momentously loud. He did not realise that his own sounds were just as loud, yet neither of them was making as much noise as he suspected.

It suddenly struck him that parents had always seemed to be so calm and unafraid, whatever the situation, and yet here they were, Jessie's parents, feeling all the emotions that he had associated only with childhood. Argus began to wonder at the apparent strength of parents. How real was it?

He wriggled on a few more paces, then paused again. Now they could clearly see the light of the fire, and the dark shapes of the bodies sitting around it. One of the shapes stood up and seemed to be coming towards them. Argus gasped and trembled. But the man went to a tree and urinated against it, then returned to the fire. Argus could hear the low voices conversing around the flames.

The boy thought that they must surely only be twenty paces away from Jessie. He felt paralysed and dry but Adious moved forward again, and that spurred him on. This time, however, they started to encounter many dry sticks, and Argus knew that the noise they were making now was inevitably going to give them away. He dragged the sling of stones around to his front, then nudged Adious, stood up and charged.

In the darkness there were hazards with every step, dead branches that kicked at ankles and reared up into knees and groins. He was aware of scattering figures at the fire, of white twisted faces turned to him in anger, of Jessie's sudden cry almost at his feet, and of Adious gathering up her daughter. Adious turned and ran, Argus made to follow, but realised that if he did they would both be swiftly caught.

He stayed where he was and plunged his hand into the sling to bring out a stone. He had a moment of even greater panic when he got his hand tangled up in the shirt and could not free the stone. Then its cool strength was in his hand and, closing his eyes at the enormity of what he was doing, he flung it with full strength at the head of one of the party coming towards him. Not at the first one, for he was so close that Argus could not find the cold-blooded power to throw it into his face. But the man he hit gave a kind of groaning gasp, raised his hands, and fell over backwards. Argus threw another stone, this time into the mouth of the man who was about to reach him. He turned and ran as he heard a gurgling scream.

He ran and ran, sobbing and talking to himself, smashing through undergrowth and obstacles. There were times when he thought he heard Adious in front of him, but it could have easily been animals that he had disturbed in his flight. It was quite a while before it dawned on him that there were no sounds from behind him. But he kept going, desperate to be clear of the area before daybreak.

He did not think about navigating until, after struggling through a particularly thick belt of vegetation, he suddenly found himself on a road. It ran north and south, but the road he wanted ran east and west. Nevertheless he took it, as a relief, and because he knew he was too far to the north anyway. And to his pleasure it soon began to curve to the south-east. He did not realise it was the road he wanted, the road he and Adious had travelled on, until he rounded a corner and saw her standing in front of him waiting warily with Jessie in her arms. He had come unexpectedly to the place they had chosen for their rendezvous.

Despite their exhaustion — which left them staggering like old people, at times not able to walk in a straight line — Argus and Adious travelled at a furious pace, to get away from the bleak district which had proved such an ominous area for them. When they finally located their campsite again they found their few possessions pillaged, and anything of value taken, but they wasted no time rueing this new misfortune. They were just grateful to be able to get on their way.

Jessie was subdued for a day or two, but quickly regained her usual good spirits and curiosity. Yet her sleep was troubled and there was a new timidity in her. She woke up at slight sounds and liked to cuddle close to Argus and Adious when they slept. Argus found he had a blackness inside him now, a black boiling part that curdled and gave off fumes when he saw Jessie's fear and thought of the shadowy people who had swept her away in the middle of the night.

It was a week before the small family felt safe enough to be able to rest. By then they were three days clear of the wastelands and in country that was lush with sky-swept grass. By a small lake they lay and slept and ate and allowed themselves to dream a little again. Though they were not yet in country that they recognised, it was nevertheless of a type familiar enough to them to suggest that they were nearing their destinations. Argus began to feel nervous and excited. He wondered if he had learnt all that he was supposed to, all that he could have learnt. In his mind he had the general outlines of most of his seven stories established, but there were many details to work out and the idea of telling them to an audience of respected elders and leaders, back in his own valley, made his legs feel a little weak.

'Do you think I've changed much?' he asked Adious.

'Oh yes,' she replied, shocked that he could even wonder.

'In what ways?' Argus persisted. Adious had to think.

'Well,' she said, chewing thoughtfully on a stick, 'I don't

know, really. All of the things I think of, when I think about them for a minute, I realise you always had, only now a little more so, if you see what I mean. I was going to say, you've become more mature and responsible, but then you were mature and responsible right from the start. Then I was going to say that you've become more interesting, with your poetry and stuff, and some of the things you say, but you were interesting right from the start too. Sometimes I think you're too serious, but just as I start thinking that you go and do something mad like this morning, pretending the clouds were kites, that you had on a string — I like your imagination. And I like your sense of humour. And I like your body.'

She began tickling Argus, who rolled over and over, giggling and fighting her off. 'Careful, you'll wake the baby', he protested. They rolled into the shallows of the lake and the tickling turned into erotic fondling — within minutes they were making love in the warm water, their bodies caressed by the rippling waves. The few clothes they had been wearing were floating around them; they had to keep pushing them away. But soon they were too intent on their own engulfing feelings to notice any distractions.

When it was over they lay in the shallows, mesmerised by the water.

'Oh,' sighed Adious, 'I don't think staying with my aunt is going to be a lot of fun.' Argus gently disengaged himself, rolled over on his back, and lay looking up at the few light clouds. He thought vaguely that a poem about voyages would be a good thing to write: about voyages across oceans and into the shallows of a lake, about voyages away from harbours and to the dark green side of the moon, voyages into Adious and into himself. He hauled himself out of the water and onto the sands, so that he could dream without drowning, and drifted away on his own weather-beaten ship, a colourful junk of patches and pictures and strange sailing people. Remembering a woman he had helped bury on a beach, he began to form words in his head.

> A vessel, fresh-launched, knows nothing
> Of how the sea behaves.
> All that it has, and all that it learns
> Comes from the wind and the reef and the waves.
> Fresh-launched, the vessel does not know
> How even a harbour harbours graves.

> A voyage that never leaves shelter
> Is one for the weak and the small.
> The strength a ship has, comes from its fight
> To weather the rips and the rocks and the squalls.
> Such a vessel, straining onwards,
> Need not fear the deep pitfalls.

Chapter Twenty-Two

Autumn had taken its first discreet initiatives as Argus trudged up the long white driveway that led home. He was tired, but his eyes scanned every detail keenly. Everything was the same, and yet everything was not the same. That walnut tree there, it still stood, and was indisputably the same tree, but a branch was missing from its lower limbs, and a ladder leaned against its trunk. Some work had been done on enlarging the dam in South Austin, but it was unfinished, and it looked as though the job had been waiting quite a time to be completed. Argus found the paradox, of familiar sights that had become unfamiliar, disconcerting. It was rather like a reunion with an old friend who had gained weight, changed his hairstyle, and now dressed differently. Such a person could never be a stranger, but could never again be the same old friend either.

Argus also found the condition of the fences worrying. His father had always told him that a farm could be judged by its fences, and here they were in a shabby state. Repairs had been made, and holes patched, but not with the high standard of workmanship that Argus had come to take for granted.

He had sometimes considered the possibility that he

might return to find his parents infirm, ill, or even dead, but this had been a hypothetical dilemma, a mere day-dream. Now the daydream merged with the reality and his anxiety heightened. He increased his pace, but knew it would be a long half-hour before he would reach the house.

It was in fact a little under twenty minutes before he came to the familiar cluster of buildings. He was impressed by his own speed and realised just how much he had grown in strength and fitness and vigour. The walk to the road had once seemed to him a major expedition: now it was a thing of no consequence. But that was something to ponder over; for the moment there was the sight that he had hungered for. In front of him was his dog, Dusty. Dusty began to bark at the apparent stranger then took a tentative step forward in an apprehension of delight, then another step as his face began to open in a beam of joy. His wonderful dream was confirmed and he leaped about in an ecstasy of barks and yelps, performing acro-batics all over and around the boy. Argus dropped to his knees, trying in vain to hug the dog, but Dusty's delirium of delight could not be contained for a moment. Argus' face was slathered with Dusty's tongue as the dog kissed him and butted him and fell all over him in a madness of love. It was a full five minutes before Argus finally found the ruthlessness to get up again and walk on towards the house, with Dusty at his heels, under his feet, or scooting around him in circles of joyful abandonment, still whining to himself in a frenzy of happiness.

Perhaps it was Dusty's noise that brought Argus' mother out of the house. At any rate she was suddenly standing on the path waiting for her son. Argus had a moment of feeling remote and alienated, then experienced a rush of warmth and love. He took her in his arms, and was staggered to see that he was now considerably taller than she was. He was amazed too to see her frailty, the greyness in her hair and the gauntness of her face. He felt a boniness in her body that had not been there before. She was trembling as they hugged but otherwise retained the calmness and dignity that had always been her hallmark. They walked together up the path. 'Your father will be glad to see you,' she said quietly. 'He hasn't been very well.'

In the cool dark of the house, smelling older than Argus had remembered it, the boy found his father sitting asleep in an armchair. His hair, for so long a proud silver, was now grey and wispy. In the relaxation of sleep his face sagged. Argus woke him gently and it took the old man a confused moment to realise what was happening.

'Ah,' he said at last. 'You've come. I knew you would.' He staggered to his feet and embraced his son, who found that he towered over this parent too. He also found that he had to support his father and after a moment he lowered him back into the armchair.

'A glass of wine, mother,' the man said. 'A glass of wine for the traveller.'

Chapter Twenty-Three

Argus was surprised, thinking about it later, to realise how quickly the three of them settled into their new relationship, with little apparent effort. There was an atmosphere in the house of sluggishness, as though the old people had been in a long sleep before he came. As Argus moved with energy and vigour through the rooms, he could feel the dormant air being disturbed, ripples emanating from his body and becoming waves. The still rooms stirred into life again.

Argus' parents were content to concede everything to their son. When he spoke they listened deferentially. Meals were served when he was hungry. When he was tired and went to bed they followed almost straight away. It was forbidden for Argus to talk about his journey until after the telling of the seven stories. His parents, traditionalists, kept to this rule; Argus quickly became reacquainted with routines on the farm. And he learnt of the changes which had occurred since he went away. His father had been ill for a long time with pneumonia, and still had little strength. Ranald, the neighbour who often worked for his father, had come as often as he could, but that was not often enough. His mother, quite a bit younger than his father, had not been ill but seemed to Argus to have aged quickly too. Argus found himself working from dawn till after dark, bringing the farm back into condition. Yet his pace was tempered by regard for his father, who accompanied him everywhere, trying to help. Argus felt that his own energy and quickness were somehow an affront to his father, an implicit insult. He forced himself to slow down, to seek his father's counsel, to include him in the work, even though he was often impatient to be getting on with it, and sure of what needed to be done.

As word spread that Argus had returned from his journey, neighbours began to call, bringing customary gifts of food. In talking with them and asking them questions Argus realised the wisdom of the rule that the journey must not be discussed with anyone until after the telling of the stories. The rule reminded the traveller, filled with the importance of his own adventure, that the experiences of the people in his home district were important too, even if they were less glamorous. It reminded him of his place in the scheme of things. While Argus had been coping with love and danger and death, these people, his neighbours, had been growing their crops, tending their cattle, raising their children and mending their fences. In other words, they too had been coping with the whole cycle of life, which included, in the natural course of events, love and danger and death. Argus saw that in many ways his journey had been unnecessary, for all the things he had encountered and learned, could have been learned here in the valley. Yet he also knew that he needed to leave the valley and make the journey in order to come to that realisation.

After he had been home a week his father went away for a few hours, and upon his return handed Argus his summons. He was to appear before the Council of the Valley, in a week's time, for seven consecutive nights. Though the summons did not say so, Argus knew that if he passed this, the great test, on the eighth night there would be feasting and a dance, to which all the people in the valley would come, as he himself had gone to others' feasts when he was younger.

He left his father and walked away, up to the steepest and most distant paddock, Yardley's, to check on a heifer that Ranald had told him was down. He was excited and nervous, yet aware of a strange feeling of detachment. Thinking it through, he realised it was because the importance of the test was not as absolute as he had once believed. Supposing he failed, what then? In the first instance there would be the embarrassment, not only to him but to his parents. There would be painful silences with friends and neighbours, for the embarrassment would often lie in the subjects which could not be raised, rather than in what was actually said. He would be excluded from the privileges and responsibilities that went with the status of adult in the valley. Certainly, as time went on, and he aged, he would be accepted as an adult anyway, but without any ceremony or sense of pride. And the position of elder would be forever closed to him. There was a boy further along the valley, Suraci, who was known to all the children as brash and shallow, a braggart. He had been away for only a short time, a few months, and had returned as cocky as ever. Argus was never told what happened when Suraci appeared before the Council — he was not entitled to know — but there had been no feast for Suraci. From then on the boy had changed completely, and had crept around the valley like a shadow of a bird on water.

But Argus knew that for him it was different. If he failed the test it would be through circumstances outside himself, and he would feel no shame. He did not need a Council of senior men and women to tell him whether he had achieved maturity or not. He knew that he had, though he would continue to gain wisdom, and to mature, through all the days of his life. And his mood was affected by the fact that he did not plan to stay in the valley long. He was anxious to go back to the town of Conroy, where he had left Adious with her aunt, and to return with her and Jessie to their own small holding. Though his resolve to do this had been weakened by the illness of his father and by the state in which he found the farm, it nevertheless remained his major priority. And when he did leave the valley, he wanted it to be with honour and dignity. For this reason the telling of the seven stories was important to him.

He could find no trace of the heifer in Yardley's, so instead he sat on the ridgeline and looked out over the farm. It was an attractive sight, and one that filled him with love for his home and his parents who had raised him here. He knew that he could not call himself an adult if he were to walk away from his responsibilities to them. Yet he also knew that if he stayed on the farm and took its management over from his father, then there would be a part of him that would never grow up. There was no malice in this. It was just the way things were, and a lot of it was to do with love — the love of parents who wished to protect their son from hazards and mistakes. Argus was clear enough about all the emotions involved but unclear about how they could be resolved. He sighed, stood up, and jogged off down the hill to check a blocked

pipe in a gravity-fed water trough. All these small jobs!
Every day was full of them. Would the time ever come
when he could walk away from them and go back to
Adious and Jessie?

Chapter Twenty-Four

On a cool autumn night, with the dark sky bewitched by stars, Argus stood in front of the Council to begin his first story. Between thirty and forty men and women were present. He knew them all, by sight or by name, and felt himself to be among friends, even though the atmosphere for this important occasion was serious and formal. His parents, both members of the Council, were debarred by custom from attending. There was dinner, a few short speeches, then Argus was introduced by his father's brother, Fahey. He stood, nervously cleared his throat, and began:

The First Story

'IN the days long ago there lived on the earth a creature called Slither. Something like a lizard, something like a snake, he had a body of immense length, so long that he did not know where it ended, and he had no idea how long it might be. His body stretched out across the plains behind him. On a clear day he could see where it disappeared through a gap in the mountains. Sometimes he would amuse himself by shrugging his shoulders and watching rocks crash down the mountains five minutes later, as ripples from the movement reached the narrow defile.

'For all his great size Slither was extraordinarily dextrous. It was nothing for him to tie his body into interesting knots. One of his amusements was to make these knots as complicated as possible and then to have the fun of unravelling them. A few times, however, he scared himself by tying knots so difficult that he began to wonder if he would ever get them untangled.

'When he was young, Slither stayed in the same area, eating the leaves and bushes that formed the main part of his diet. He ate quite a lot, because if he went for very long without eating he began to get signals from a distant part of his body that it was hungry and wanted nourishment. Before he was very old he had eaten out most of the plains on which he lived and was obliged to move on. He travelled as smoothly as he could but it was inevitable that the passage of his body across the countryside caused a lot of disruption, especially as it took him years to pass any one spot. He travelled across oceans, which was easy for him, as most of his body was still waiting on the shore when he reached the other side. And he hardly noticed the tidal waves that he generated as he made the crossing.

'One day, when journeying in a new continent. Slither came across a remarkable discovery. It was a giant barrier that crossed his path from east to west. Slither had never seen anything like it. In size it resembled a mountain range, yet it was made of materials that were not like any mountains he had ever seen. It was a kind of scaly substance, made up of many colours, and quite beautiful when the sunlight was reflecting from it. It was firm to touch but gave when prodded. At times it seemed as though a trembling movement would run right along it.

'Slither became fascinated by this remarkable barrier. Though he could have slid over it quite easily, he chose not to. He looked to the left, where it disappeared into the west, and he looked to the right, where it disappeared into the east. He decided to follow it to the east, to see where it led.

'That was the start of a long pilgrimage by Slither. It was a strange time in his life. He ate hardly at all, and his body — as much of it as he could see — became scrawny and thin. He did not even notice the countryside that he was passing through, and would not have known at any given moment whether he was in jungle or grassland or forest. He did much more damage to the land and its inhabitants than ever before because he had become careless about the way in which he travelled. He was obsessed by his quest, to explore the full length of this strange phenomenon that he had found.

'As he slid along beside it, Slither did notice that the mountain range — if indeed that was what it was — was becoming smaller and meaner and less attractive. He began to feel that he might be disappointed in what he found at the end of this rainbow. But even though he was getting weary and dispirited he pressed on.

'The time came when Slither felt that he was approaching the end of the search. He had an instinct that there was not long to go. At the same time, he began to feel that there was something very familiar about the part that he was now journeying beside. He could not place exactly what it was, but there was something about it that he felt he recognised.

'At last came the moment when all his questions were answered. After a few hours of exhausted sleep one night Slither woke at the first shadowing of greyness in the sky. He moved off again straight away, travelled a very short distance, and then, as the sun rose, found himself looking at his own emaciated neck. The barrier he had been travelling beside all this time, was his own body, and he had been depriving himself of everything to do this. There was now only one comfort for Slither — that at least he had recognised in the end what his obsession had been. Otherwise he might still be absorbed in his fruitless journey.'

Argus sat down quietly, as he had been taught. Some minutes of murmured discussion among his audience followed, but, as he had been warned, no looks or comments were directed towards him. In time his uncle rose, and gestured for Argus to follow him. Fahey led him out of the meeting place, and walked him home across the soft wet paddocks, saying nothing to him, except for a parting admonition to be ready at the same time the next night. Argus went to bed and lay for a long time looking out of his window, at the stars that so brilliantly punctured the sky.

The Second Story

'NEAR the town of Perno,' Argus began, 'was a river which ran deep but which could be forded in places if one was careful. At one of the fords lived a man named Sussan. He had placed a rope across the river to aid those who wished to cross. The traffic at this particular ford was quite heavy, as it was on a direct route between Perno and Capital, so people liked its convenience, even though it was one of the more dangerous crossings. But people didn't mind getting a bit wet if it saved them time.

'One day the river was flowing swiftly; it was dirty, and had risen a good way because of heavy rainfalls further upstream. A man called Marne came to the river with his wife and children. To the wife, the river seemed dangerous and she told her husband that they should walk up to the next ford and try to cross there instead. The children were not really old enough to assess the situation for themselves but, seeing that their mother was disturbed by the height of the water, they supported her pleas and promised their father that they would not complain about the extra walk. But Marne was a stubborn man and, with the rope to hold on to, he was sure there would be no danger. He told his family he would cross first and then they could follow.

'As he began to wade into the water Sussan came out of his hut and watched. Marne was already so far advanced in his course that Sussan felt it was futile to try to recall the man. He watched with increasing fear as Marne, with water up to his waist already, approached the centre of the river. Suddenly a new wall of frothy water swept downstream and knocked Marne off balance. It almost dragged the heavy pack from the man's back and Marne reached around in an attempt to get it back onto his shoulders. In doing so he lost his grip on the rope and was swept under. He did not surface again and, although his wife and children and Sussan ran along the banks of the river for quite a way, hoping to find him a mile or more downstream, it was not until the river subsided a week or so later that his body was found, trapped under a log-jam.'

Argus paused in his story and looked around. The drowning of the foolish man was not the point of the tale as his listeners knew. Argus continued.

'When the wife returned to her home in Capital, she had to tell the story of her husband's death many times to her friends and neighbours and relatives. She did not want to give her husband a bad name by making him sound foolish or lazy, so she explained to them all that he crossed the river because the children were so tired from the long walk that they could not walk the extra distance involved. "Even though they offered to go round the long way," she would say to people, "we knew that their little legs would find the journey too far."

'The children also found themselves telling the story; not just when they were young, but again and again over the years, to new friends and acquaintances. The oldest child, a boy, had a vivid memory of watching his father's face in the water as the man was swept downstream, and he incorporated this dramatic fact into his rendition; and, as time passed, he began to fancy that his father had called out to him as well. The words he imagined that his father had called out were, "My son, my son". The second child heard her mother's story about the children being too tired to go a safer way and she felt very guilty, as though she were responsible for her father's death. When she told the story she seemed to remember a remorseful conversation in which her father had told her she was a lazy little girl, and had then plunged into the water in a bad temper. The last child was too young to remember the actual tragedy, so his version of the events was a colourful one involving a rope bridge breaking and a number of travellers being swept away.

'Back at the ford, Sussan sometimes recounted to passing travellers the story of the drowning of Marne. Indeed it became a popular story over the years, and people often asked for it. Sussan would describe a violent argument with the doomed man, where he, Sussan, would be knocked to the ground in his attempts to stop Marne from dashing suicidally into the swollen river. Marne would then be pictured clinging to the rope as Sussan made frantic efforts to reach him, with poles or a length of rope. Just as his desperate, white fingers clutched at the end of the pole a gust of water knocked him loose and with a despairing look he was sucked away to his death. Sussan did not have to tell the story many times before he began to believe in it himself, as did all the other actors in the drama, whenever they told their different accounts. They could see the drowning man's face, could remember the words that his lips formed, could even remember how they felt as they relived events that never happened.

'Many years later Marne's wife came through the ford again. By then a bridge had been built, but Sussan still lived there. Indeed he had prospered, having built a store and a guest house by the crossing. Marne's widow stayed in the guest house and after dinner she was privileged to hear Sussan, in the midst of stories about the old days, tell of the drowning of her husband. But the story had changed so much that she did not recognise it. She only thought sadly of the many tragedies that the river must have seen, and, not having recognised Sussan, wished that he could have been there when her husband attempted his fatal crossing. "For", she thought, "we did not try hard enough to dissuade him from going, and perhaps we could have done more to help him when he was washed under."'

Argus paused, having almost finished his story. 'By the way,' he added, 'that's not what really happened. Marne caught cold from crossing the river and died two weeks later from pneumonia. But his children like to believe it was more dramatic than that. That is, if he had any children. And the bit at the end about Marne's widow hearing the story and not recognising it — I just put that in to make a point.'

His listeners laughed heartily with him and Argus knew they had understood, and liked, the story.

The Third Story

ARGUS said: 'There was once a field containing many flowers, all of a small blue type. These flowers were unusual, in that they could come into bloom in any season of the year. At any given time there would be some flowers in the field that were very old — almost withered away — and some that would be in full flower, and others that were still folded buds.' Argus used his hands to sketch in the air the shape of the new buds. 'And,' he continued, 'there were butterflies in the field that were always in motion. They would land first on one flower, then on another. It didn't matter what stage the flower was at; the butterflies didn't care. They didn't understand "forwards" or "backwards", or even straight lines. They just kept going from flower to flower.' He paused.

'The field,' he said carefully, 'is called Time. And the butterflies, the butterflies are us.'

The Fourth Story

'ONCE upon a time there lived a girl by the name of Alzire. She was a solitary child who lived near a great hill named Goffa. Every night, as dusk fell, she would climb to the top of this high hill and there she would fly, on the end of a very long string, a star that she had made. The star would be cold and white during the day, when she kept it in a cupboard in her bedroom, but as night approached it would begin to pulsate with colour and life, and glow with warmth. It seemed to take on a life of its own. Every night it would join the millions of other stars in the sky, even though on cloudy or stormy nights Alzire would not be able to see it as it soared high above her in the heavens. But she did not mind its invisibility on these occasions: she was more than compensated on the other nights when her star proudly took its place in the glittering display. As she watched it and felt it tugging on the string, it seemed to her as though the sky were like music and her star an essential note in a concert of triumph.

'Cold nights and warm nights were all the same to Alzire. Every night she stood on her hill, faithfully flying the kite until the greying of the sky told her that dawn was calling in the stars and the cold white moon. Often she would pass the time thinking about the many other solitary figures like herself, all around the world, each standing on his or her own hilltop, each with a bright star on a long string. She felt a great love for them, as though they were all joined in a network of friendship.

'One night, when she was about thirteen, Alzire set off for the hill of Goffa a little before dusk, as she always did. Climbing the hill with her head down, body bent forward and the star under her arm, she did not see until she was nearly at the top that something had changed. Suddenly her way was blocked by a huge shadow. Alzire knew every plant, every rock, every smudge of dirt on the path, and she knew that this shadow did not belong. She stopped and looked up. Straddling the top of the hill, staring down at her, was a dark and monstrous shape, so black that it was impossible to tell where the shadow ended and reality began. It appeared to be a living thing, for it had eyes, any number of them, and all focused on her. Alzire shivered and shook. She could not move from the spot where she stood. At last, realising that she could not stay there forever, and a little comforted by the fact that the monster had not moved, she began backing slowly away. As she did so the baleful gaze of those terrible eyes remained fixed upon her, until a bend in the path took her trembling legs around a corner, and she found herself out of sight of the thing. And then she turned and ran for home.

'All night Alzire tossed and turned, not only for fear of the creature that was on Goffa, but also in distress at the absence of her star from the night sky. She got up and sat at the window for hours, looking out at the brightly splattered heavens. All those stars and hers not among them! She could not sleep, and morning found her in an unhappy state. She kept the star on her bed, where it glowed dimly, casting a faint light on the walls and ceiling of her room.

'The next night Alzire climbed the hill again, but with none of her usual confidence. And her worst fears were realised. When she came to the same bend in the path she looked up with a sense of foreboding, to see, once again, the great monster in the same position as the night before, though if anything it now seemed even bigger. It was crouched over the top of Goffa, in a position from which it could easily launch an attack, and the bulk of its vast body covered the whole summit. Alzire could now distinguish its head from the dark shadows that surrounded it. The head was big as a house and was mounted on a neck that was long and supple as a reptile's body. Slowly the girl retreated again and returned to her house for another sleepless night.

'This pattern was repeated for seven nights. Alzire was becoming desperate, and thought even of sacrificing her life in a mad rush at the creature. Every night her star grew a little dimmer, as though the monster was sapping light from it. Alzire began to fear that it would go out forever.

'On the eighth day Alzire found herself in the garden, watching the gardener at work. The gardener, an old gentle woman, called Alzire over.

'"Look at this," she said, pointing to a leaf. Alzire walked listlessly over and peered at it. She saw a cocoon, with something gradually emerging from it. As the insect chewed its way clear Alzire realised that it was a little black wasp.

'"I thought that was a caterpillar's cocoon," she said in surprise. "Look, that's a caterpillar's skin right next to it."

'"Ah yes," said the gardener. "The caterpillar thought so too. But before the caterpillar even lost its first skin, it had a visitor. You see, this type of wasp lays its egg straight into the caterpillar. The egg hatches and the baby grub gets its nourishment by eating the inside of the cater-

175

pillar. Not that he knows about it; he goes on eating, too, and getting bigger, but in the end he's no match for the wasp larva inside him. By the time that last skin came off it was the wasp that shed it, as there was nothing left of the caterpillar. Then the wasp-grub makes its own cocoon and settles down for a while to grow into a fully-fledged wasp."

'"That's horrible!" Alzire exclaimed. "That's terrible!"

'"Oh, it happens all the time," the gardener said mildly. "That, and things like it. Happens with humans too in a way. We nourish evil things inside us, and eventually they destroy us if we let them, and then out they come, triumphant and powerful. Yes, we make our own monsters." She looked knowingly at the girl, then turned back to her work.

'With a great flash of understanding Alzire suddenly understood what the gardener was telling her. The creature on Goffa was her own creation, born out of her own darkness. It had fed on her moments of selfishness and weakness for all these years and finally it had grown strong enough to survive on its own — and to destroy her star. The girl realised that this was her moment of decision; that unless she could destroy the monster now, she would be trapped forever.

'She ran into the house to find a weapon. But although she searched the contents of every room, there was nothing with the aura of power that she sought. It was not until the late afternoon that she came again to her bedroom and there saw on the bed the only thing strong enough to help her. Taking the star on its string, she set off towards the hill of Goffa once more, but this time with hope and determination in her heart. She did not even see the old woman, the gardener, who watched her go.

'Alzire climbed the mountain, gaining strength from the fact that the star glowed brighter with every step she took. As she rounded the final curve in the path once more she saw the grim creature waiting for her, but this time she felt no fear. Raising the star she started towards the shadowy monster. But as the light fell upon the top of the mountain, the shadows retreated, and the monster seemed to shrink and shrink. The darkness faded before the light. Alzire realised how much power the thing had drawn from her fear; how much fear had magnified its size. When she finally confronted it, on the very top of the storm-tossed hill of Goffa, she was surprised to see how small it really was. But when she raised her hand to strike it, it slipped away, and bounded down through the long grass, disturbing rocks and small stones as it went. It was quickly out of sight.

'It was then, with her new understanding, that Alzire became aware this creature could never be killed, but only kept as small as possible, and stopped from growing. To keep it so small as to be insignificant was perhaps the greatest and most important task that life offered. With a sense of responsibility very different from the light-hearted way in which she had flown her kite before, Alzire unfurled the string and let it soar back into the heavens where it belonged. The star seemed to almost burst with light. And it seemed to Alzire that every other star in the firmament was glowing more brightly than ever before, as if each and every one of them was saying: "Welcome brother! Welcome sister! Welcome at last!"'

The Fifth Story

'THE world's greatest circus,' Argus began, his voice and delivery showing signs of greater confidence, 'was always laid out in the form of an avenue. Its owner, a woman named Zexta, had a fine sense of climax. She liked to begin with the smaller acts, to whet the crowd's appetite. They would pay their money and enter at one end of the avenue, where they would see twisters and rumblers and bouncers. As they went on a little further they would be invited to watch acrobats and stilt-walkers. Beyond them, they would linger at the scrabblers and contortionists.

'As the people made their way along the avenue, however, they would become conscious of a huge pavilion that was waiting for them at the end of it. Zexta, with her magnificent sense of showmanship, had designed it so that it was higher and broader than all the other buildings. She had it draped in curtains, a kind of heavy silver brocade, so that it was always in the corner of people's eyes. And it was resplendent with banners, all of which bore the same message in different words: "SEE THE FREAK", "ABSOLUTELY THE ONLY ONE IN THE WORLD", "A UNIQUE BEING", "POSSIBLY THE MOST AMAZING CREATURE IN CREATION".

'So while the people were looking at the roller-boarders and the wobblers, they would also be thinking about the pavilion at the end of the avenue, and speculating about what kind of oddity might be in it. By the time they reached it they had convinced themselves — or rather, Zexta had convinced them — that they were going to see something truly extraordinary. As indeed they were.

'Access to the pavilion was by way of a large set of solid steps. People mounted these and then walked along a ramp which started wide but kept narrowing, so that eventually everyone was forced into single file. At this point they passed through the entrance, viewed the freak within, and then were ushered on through an exit which took them right out on to the street, leaving the circus behind.

'And what did they see? Who was the freak?' Argus smiled. 'They saw a unique creature all right. For Zexta had placed nothing but a huge mirror in her splendid pavilion.'

The Sixth Story

'A BOY once lived in a certain place. There were things there. When he was hungry he put things in his mouth and his hunger went away. When he was cold he put things on his body and the cold was gone. When he was tired he closed his eyes and lay down, and something would happen for some time, and the tiredness would be ended.

'One day he heard an old voice talking. The voice kept talking about a "garden". The boy thought this was a very pleasant word. There was something beautiful about it, that caught hold inside him and would not let go. So he decided to go and find this thing called a "garden". He began to walk, looking for this thing.

'He walked a long way and did not find any "garden". But one evening, at around dusk, he heard a sound that he thought the most fragrant and delicate he had ever heard. It shivered and tingled around him in the twilight.

179

The sound seemed to come from a young girl, and near her was sitting an old woman.

'The boy said to the woman, "What is that sound?"

'The woman answered, "It is the sound of a flute, playing music."

'The boy said, "It is very beautiful."

'"Yes," the woman answered, "It is something like the sound of birds in a garden."

'The boy travelled on, until one day he came to a huge and ornate palace. He went inside, into a great hall, at the end of which was a man dressed in robes. The boy walked towards him, marvelling at the soft feel of the floor beneath his bare feet.

'The boy said to the man, "What a wonderful thing this is to walk on!"

'"Yes," said the man, who was a king. "It is called carpet. It is rather like the grass that one finds in a garden."

'The boy went on his way, still searching. Some time later he met a woman carrying a large square thing under her arm.

'"May I see what you are carrying?" the boy asked politely. The woman held it up for the boy to see, and he was struck dumb with astonishment. He had never seen anything so exquisite.

'"What is it?" he asked faintly, when he had got his voice back.

'"It is a painting of a flower," the woman replied. "A flower from a garden."

'The very next day the boy came upon a group of people all seated around a table, laughing and talking. They were putting different things into their mouths. In particular, they were dipping their hands into a large jar that stood in the centre of the table, then they sucked on their fingers. The boy sat down with them but they seemed not to notice him. After a while he was emboldened to follow their example with the large jar. As soon as he transferred the stuff to his lips, his mouth was filled with a rich glow of great sweetness. It was as though the flute was now playing in his mouth.

'"What is this?" he asked the people in delight.

'They turned their faces to him.

'"It is honey," they answered.

'"What is honey?" he asked.

'"It comes from the nectar of flowers," they explained. "Out of nectar the bees make honey."

'Much later on his travels the boy met a beautiful young girl, dressed in white, walking beside an expanse of water. The boy went up to her, sure that he could learn from someone so attractive. As he approached her he felt a wonderful sensation fill his head: he felt that it was lifting him from the ground. He realised that this feeling was entering his head through his nose, and he touched his nose dazedly.

'"What is happening to me?" he asked.

'"Perhaps it is my perfume," the girl said shyly.

'"Perfume?" the boy queried.

'"Yes, perfume," the girl said. "Perfume is our poor attempt to distil the smells of Nature into a liquid, so we can carry the smells around with us wherever we go."

'Filled with wonder at the things he had learned, the boy was more determined than ever to find a garden, and so he searched all the harder. But his searching was in vain. No matter how hard he tried he could not find it. After a long long time he was at last forced to abandon his quest and return home. He walked with head hanging low and feet dragging in the dust. But as he came to his home once more, something wonderful happened. He heard the clear musical sounds of birds singing. He smelt the sweet richness of flowers growing. He felt the soft coolness of grass under his feet. He lifted his head and saw the colours staggering with joy, the wise shade of great trees, the bright movement of bees. "This is a garden," he exclaimed with delight. "All the time I had a garden here at home, but I had to go away to understand it!"'

The Seventh Story

ARGUS crossed his fingers that he would remember and hoped that he was not straying so far outside the guidelines that he would offend the elders. He took a deep breath.

> He walked with his feet on a roadway,
> A path that was clearly defined.
> But the journey that really had meaning
> Was the one that took place in his mind.
>
> Whenever he came to a crossroad
> He had his choices to make.
> But his legs played no part in choosing
> Which of the roads he must take.
>
> Wisdom lay not in his muscles
> Nor in the soles of his feet.
> It came from the light of achievement,
> It came from the mud of defeat.

THE JOURNEY

The further one walks, the more crossroads.
And the harder the choices become.
In country that's strange or unfriendly
The ignorant soon will succumb.

And there's four different paths to be taken
None can be safely ignored.
Even the one that's been travelled
Needs to be further explored.

For there's always a road to friendship
And there's always a road to fame
And there's always a road to danger
— And a road that wants walking again.

Chapter Twenty-Five

A week after the celebrations, when the stream of well-wishers had at last started to dry up, Argus faced his parents again, in a curious replay of his first departure from home. He had told them much about his journey, including a detailed account of his life with Adious. They had listened anxiously and his father had commented at the end, 'You weren't meant to grow up that much'. His mother said nothing. Argus realised from his father's comment that although he had changed, his parents had not. It helped to make him feel easier in his mind about the course he must now take. And so he told them that it was time for him to set off once more, to meet up with Adious and Jessie, and that he did so not only out of a sense of commitment but also out of love.

But before he had finished, his mother was silently weeping and his father's lips too were quivering.

'I'm sorry,' Argus said gently, feeling a little desperate. 'But hear me out, please. I've got two suggestions to make, and I want you to agree to one of them before I go. The first one is that Adious and Jessie and I come and winter with you every year. We'd be happy to do that and it would mean that you could save all the major jobs on the farm until I got here each year, so that the place could be kept in good shape. But the other idea is that you retire from the farm here and come with us to our valley. It's small but it's pretty, and I'd build you a house where you'd get lots of sunlight. It's a peaceful place, and you could do as much or as little work as you wanted. The only thing that I wouldn't excuse you from is playing with Jessie, and teaching her as you taught me.'

There was a long silence in the room.

'It'd be hard for us to leave our friends here,' Argus' father finally said.

'Yes, I know,' Argus said, not attempting to cover the problem with platitudes.

'What's the night sky like?' his mother asked, thinking of her astronomy.

'Rich in stars,' Argus answered, smiling. There was another long silence, which Argus broke. 'It's something to think about,' he said. 'There's no rush. I plan to leave around the end of the week, to get Adious. If you think you might be interested, then we'd come back here from Conroy, to talk it over some more, and to move you, if that's what you decide you want. But,' he added, in unconscious imitation of the words he often wished his parents had said to him, 'you decide what's right for you. Whatever suits you best.'

It was, as it turned out, a little over a week before Argus actually left. During that time he knew that his parents had many anxious discussions about his proposal. They asked him a number of questions, but it was hard for him to tell whether they were starting to favour the move or not. But they did at least intimate that they wanted to meet Adious, and so it was agreed that he would return with her and Jessie as soon as he had paid his respects to the aunt in Conroy.

In the event he was not away for long. This time they heard him before they saw him, as he came whooping and singing up the driveway, with a dusty, smiling Adious and an excited Jessie riding on his back.

'Pack your bags, grandma!' he shouted out to his parents as they came out to greet the little family. 'Get your things, grandpa. We're looking for a midwife and a couple of grandparents. It's going to be a springtime baby and we want you there to see it!'

With another exultant whoop he slipped Jessie off his back and began turning cartwheels around the verandah. His parents looked at each other then at Adious, and the three of them smiled, the smile of loving complicity. Argus grabbed his mother around the waist and began dancing with her.

'I thought we sent him away to grow up,' his father grumbled, half to himself. He looked at Adious. 'Mind you, I remember doing handstands along this verandah the night he was born. Ah well, I guess somehow none of us ever grow up.'

He turned, and with a new sense of life in his step, went inside to fetch a bottle of wine.

John Marsden
Out of Time

James reads by his open bedroom window at night.
Other lives and other worlds beckon. One of these
worlds is conjured by old Mr Woodforde, a physicist
who looks more like an accountant and who
constructs a strange black box.

One day when James slips into the laboratory, he
makes a dreadful discovery and learns to master a
great power.

Who is the little boy in Mexico who scratches pictures
of aeroplanes in the dust? How will the girl caught in
a wartime bomb blast be reunited with her parents?
And why does James sit alone in his island of silence?

With *Out of Time* John Marsden has produced a novel
that will further enhance his reputation as one of the
most successful writers of fiction for teenagers. This
is a challenging novel which poses a new question on
every page as it draws us into an ever-widening series
of mysteries, into magical, dangerous worlds– in and
out of time.

John Marsden
Letters from the Inside

Dear Tracey
I don't know why I'm answering your ad, to be
honest. It's not like I'm into pen pals, but it's a boring
Sunday here, wet, everyone's out, and I thought it'd
be something different...

Dear Mandy
Thanks for writing. You write so well, much better
than me. I put the ad in for a joke, like a dare, and
yours was the only good answer...

Two teenage girls. An innocent beginning to
friendship. Two complete strangers who get to know
each other a little better each time a letter is written
and answered.

Mandy has a dog with no name, an older sister, a
creepy brother, and some boy problems. Tracey has
a horse, two dogs and a cat, an older sister and
brother, and a great boyfriend. They both have hopes
and fears...and secrets.

As Mandy and Tracey swap confidences and share
the ups and downs of school, home and friends, they
get to know every detail of each other's lives.

Or do they?

A powerful, compelling novel from the award-winning
author of *So Much to Tell You.*

John Marsden
Take My Word For It

You know what Tracey said to me after English today? She said: 'The reason you've got no friends is that you don't tell anyone your problems' ...I hate the way they tell everyone every single detail about themselves... If you ask me, it's dangerous. Once you start, you don't stop.

Strong, cold, private...this is Lisa, as seen by Marina in her journal, *So Much to Tell You*.

But Lisa too keeps a journal. It's a record of her friends and family, her frustrations and successes, her thoughts and feelings. As page follows page, the real Lisa begins to emerge. Not always strong, not always private and certainly not cold.

If I could say what I wanted to, if I could bring it out of myself in words, this paper would be buried under the weight of it.

Take My Word For It is Lisa's story and more. It's the story of Marina, a girl struggling to find her voice among the turmoil of life in a Year 9 dormitory. It's the story of Cathy, of Kate, of Sophie.

As in the best-selling *So Much to Tell You*, award-winning novelist John Marsden takes us into the world of young people trying to make sense of their lives.